LASZLO

SEALs of Steel, Book 5

Dale Mayer

LASZLO: SEALS OF STEEL, BOOK 5
Dale Mayer
Valley Publishing Ltd.

Copyright © 2018

ISBN-13: 978-1-773360-82-9
Print Edition

About This Book

When an eight-man unit hit a landmine, all were injured but one died. The remaining seven aim to see Mouse's death avenged.

As a child, Minx's best friend was Mouse. She hasn't heard from him in years, but she's never forgotten him.

Laszlo wonders if the whole unit was targeted, or just their youngest, newest member? Minx may be the only person who knew the boy that later became a dangerous, hunted man…

Your Free Book Awaits!

KILL OR BE KILLED

Part of an elite SEAL team, Mason takes on the dangerous jobs no one else wants to do – or can do. When he's on a mission, he's focused and dedicated. When he's not, he plays as hard as he fights.

Until he meets a woman he can't have but can't forget. Software developer, Tesla lost her brother in combat and has no intention of getting close to someone else in the military. Determined to save other US soldiers from a similar fate, she's created a program that could save lives. But other countries know about the program, and they won't stop until they get it – and get her.

Time is running out ... For her ... For him ... For them ...

DOWNLOAD a ***complimentary*** copy of MASON? Just tell me where to send it!

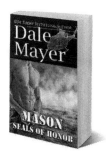

http://dalemayer.com/sealsmason/

PROLOGUE

LASZLO JENSEN WATCHED as Talon, his good arm bandaged, and Clary, her face a colorful mix of bruises, walked into Badger's house. Clary was shy, standing almost as if a part of Talon. Like everybody already knew and judged her for their tortured past. Badger stepped forward on his crutches, Dotty the coonhound on his heels with her tail wagging, and said, "There you are."

Clary smiled and reached up and gave Badger a hug. He hugged her back gently. Talon hadn't shared much about Clary's past with Badger, but he didn't need those details to understand how hard it was to heal what she'd been through. But since she'd moved into Talon's, the two of them had had lots of time to work through their differences and to get comfortable being in the same space again. And now it was as if they'd never been apart.

With everyone seated in the living room of Badger's house, Laszlo settled back, loving the feeling of having his friends grow and become a bigger, stronger family than even what they were before. Badger was moving, though slowly. It would be a long time before he would get a prosthetic back. Kat, at his side always, doted on him.

Laszlo knew they would have some badass prosthetics coming their way when the time was right. And he couldn't wait. Laszlo glanced around at the group and said, "It's good to see everybody here again."

"Except not everybody's here," Erick said. "Jager's missing. He's still dark."

"Do we know for sure he's even alive?"

Erick nodded. "I got another message. But it was simple. He's still hunting."

"He always was a bit of a loner," Laszlo said. "If he'd at least check in with us, we'd have a chance to tell him what information we have."

Geir sat on the far side of the room. "He's a good man. And when he's hunting, there's no one else like him. But I wish to hell I was out there hunting with him."

Erick nodded. "And what we have to figure out is, what's happening next. The meeting's here for Badger's sake. As he's not supposed to be moving as much as he is right now."

Badger waved his arm. "I'm fine."

Kat reached over and laced her fingers with his.

Laszlo smiled. "With Kat at your side, it's no wonder you're fine."

There was some good-humored ribbing, which Badger accepted with a smile. "She's the best thing that's happened to me." His gaze locked on Laszlo. "Did you ever notice the similarity between our group and Mason's and Levi's?"

Laszlo winced. "Hell no."

Erick and Talon chuckled. "Well, you should. Because you're next."

Cade had stayed quiet in the corner, Faith at his side, a couple beers opened between the two of them. "It's all right, Laszlo. When you're ready, it'll happen."

Laszlo shook his head. "What I'm ready for is to find this asshole."

"We're doing a full workup on Mouse," Erick said, returning to the business at hand. "We're tracking down anyone he was in contact with. And, I have to admit, it's not much. So I suggest what we do right now is everybody tell me everything they might have heard or knew about Mouse. I thought I knew him pretty well. But honestly, when I tried to dredge up some memories, it was a lot of ribbing and teasing and bugging. I thought his family was from Texas. As far as I knew, he only had a mother."

Cade leaned forward, a frown on his face. "That can't be right. I swear to God he was from California and that he lived with his parents before hitting the military."

Badger looked at the two of them. "Really?"

Erick glanced over at him. "What do you remember?"

Badger frowned. "I was closer to him than all of you. I thought he had only an uncle in Texas. But I don't remember Mouse being very willing to talk about him."

"Do you remember why?" Laszlo asked.

"No, but he was pretty adamant. I just can't remember if he gave me a specific reason or not. The thing about Mouse was, he always made up stories. It was pretty hard to tell what was real and what wasn't," Badger admitted. "But he was young. He was trying hard to be one of us, though weaker than we were. He would turn into a hell of a man and be a great member of the unit, but we all knew he wasn't quite there yet."

The men nodded.

"That's true," Geir said. "We covered for him a lot, and we helped him to make the grade as many times as we could. But he always knew he wasn't as good as the rest of us."

"But we never bugged him about it," Cade said.

And again the men nodded in agreement.

Erick wondered about that. "Do you think he wrote to his uncle, or whoever in his world who's trying to get back at us, that we were less than supportive?"

That topic brought up silence all around.

"He might have," Talon admitted. "Any teasing we did was in the same vein as teasing we always did. It was light-hearted, and we never meant any of the insults. It was the way of the world—our world particularly," Talon said. "He always was pale. Remember that?" he added with a crooked grin. "We used to tease him about spending more time in the sun to gain a bit of color."

"I remember that, and he hated coffee. He's the only one of us who didn't drink coffee." Erick smiled with the memories. The others all pitched him with bits and pieces they knew as Erick wrote it all down. He realized it was all disjointed, and nobody had a clear sense of Mouse's early beginnings. "Do you think he did that on purpose?"

"Did what?" Laszlo asked.

"Deliberately shrouded his history. Or maybe created different histories in order to make himself feel better about his life?"

"He didn't have an easy childhood, I know that," Badger said suddenly. "His body was quite scarred."

The men frowned, thinking about that.

"Did he go into the navy to escape, do you think?" Kat asked.

Badger shrugged. "I wouldn't be at all surprised."

"And then the question becomes, get away from what?" Kat asked.

Badger said quietly, "Every time I rack my brain to think of someone Mouse might have mentioned on his leaves, my mind draws a blank."

"What about girlfriends?" Clary asked. Her question landed in the middle of the group like a stone in a pond. Almost as if ripples of shock moved outward continuously.

Laszlo studied her for a long moment. "Mouse was gay."

She raised her eyebrows. "That could not have been easy in the military."

He shook his head. "Not only was it not easy, he took a lot of razzing because of it. Not from us," he assured her hurriedly. "But from a lot of the other guys."

"So maybe you guys weren't all targeted," she said quietly.

"Maybe Mouse was," Kat interjected. "How bad was it for somebody like Mouse?"

The men exchanged glances.

"Hard to say," Erick stated. "Likely bad. The navy isn't known to be easy on those who are different …"

"Suicidally bad?" asked Honey, her voice soft, gentle. "I'm sure the comments and actions would have hurt him inside, even if he didn't let anyone see his reaction."

Erick shrugged. "We never asked him about his sexuality, that I know of." He glanced around the room. "At least I didn't. Did anyone here?"

All the men shook their heads.

"No, we never did," Badger said.

"So, if he didn't have any girlfriends, what do you know about his boyfriends?" Clary asked. "Because, if it wasn't a family member, we already know it's somebody who feels very strongly about Mouse. And that means, it's usually a lover. Do you guys know who loved Mouse? Did he have anybody in his life? Did he have a permanent relationship, even an off-and-on relationship?" She turned to stare at them. "Surely, if you were all best friends and you know so much about each other, you'd know as much about Mouse?"

One by one they all turned toward each other, then cast their gazes downward.

"He didn't talk to us," Badger said quietly. "I don't think he was ashamed as much as he was afraid of being humiliated or embarrassed, like he always had been."

"How long was he with you before the accident?"

Laszlo sighed. "One year. And in that year we couldn't convince him that he was safe with us."

"But obviously he wasn't safe," Talon said quietly. "Not when he's the only one dead."

Laszlo asked, "So where do I go next?"

"You?" Talon asked. "Why you?"

"Because you're laid up. Plus Erick remains command central. And Badger is on sick leave for months to come to save what's left of his leg. So I'm the one who'll lead this next mission," he snapped. "And I'm totally okay if Geir comes along. But where are we going?"

"Texas," Erick said. "If that's where Mouse is from."

"Done," Laszlo said. "I'll head to Texas and find out for sure."

"And then what?" Clary asked.

"And then we'll start tearing poor Mouse's life apart," Laszlo said. "Way deeper than we have done so far."

She nodded. "When you find whoever loves him, go easy. It's hard to lose someone you care about."

Laszlo's smile was diamond hard. "So very true. But it's also no excuse to go around killing others who loved him too."

CHAPTER 1

L ASZLO PULLED HIS truck off the highway and took another look at the GPS. Erick and Badger had finally tracked down a potential childhood home address for Mouse. "Dallas is forty-five minutes away, and we're heading to the far side of the city."

"We didn't have to drive all this way. We could have done all of it online," Geir said quietly beside him.

"We could have, but I thought a road trip would be nice. I was getting a little hemmed in. All that inactivity was starting to bite."

"Oh, I agree with you. But you've been shifting in the driver's seat all this time."

"Yeah, I am," Laszlo said. "Out of all the injuries I sustained, the damn back is the worst. It doesn't like me sitting too long."

"You had several surgeries to correct the alignment, didn't you?"

"And several rods put in." Laszlo nodded. "Most of the time it's fine. Long drives, not so much."

"So why did we drive again?"

"Because the doctor said I need to build up that muscle tone. Not sure he meant this long of a drive, but it hasn't been too bad." Turning off the motor, Laszlo hopped out and walked around to Geir's side, shaking out his legs. "I just have to take things a bit at a time."

Geir snorted and remained in his seat, waiting until Laszlo got back in again. "We finally found an address for Mouse's family," he said, looking at his notes, "but we don't have a last-known residence from two years ago. I find that odd."

"Me too. The navy should have had that when he first signed up. Hence the road trip. Let's get to the bottom of who Mouse was. He didn't deserve what he got, but, at this point, it seems like he's got to be the center of all this."

"I don't think we can narrow our thinking to just that," Geir said. "We have to keep in mind that, although Mouse died, all of us could have from the land mine, either immediately or before any help arrived. Any of us could have died in the aftermath through our manifold surgeries. Maybe Mouse was the one who was supposed to be saved. Maybe nobody was supposed to be safe. What we don't want to do is block off our thinking to such a narrow focus that we never find the truth by asking the wrong questions or looking in only one direction."

"That's not happening," Laszlo said. "The truth is way too important." Laszlo returned, sat behind the wheel of the vehicle, leaving the door open and his legs hanging out for a minute while he rolled his neck and shoulders. With some of the tension easing, he twisted around until he faced forward again. "You need lunch?"

"I will soon," Geir said. "But food doesn't taste the same."

"Stomach problems?"

"All of it."

Laszlo nodded but didn't push the issue. Geir had ruptured his stomach and several feet of small intestine and his spleen. His liver had been badly damaged but had finally recuperated. He had a lot of internal scarring, his healing below the surface.

Whereas Laszlo's left hand had been badly burned. The scars were so disfiguring that he usually wore a glove to avoid drawing undue attention. And that was just part of his injuries. "You lost a kidney too, didn't you?"

"Yeah, I did."

No self-pity, no emotion at all. Just a fact. And again Laszlo understood. They were the walking wounded. Survivors of something they weren't meant to survive. But it showed the vitality of the human spirit and the ability of the human body to heal against all odds.

Laszlo pulled back into traffic, following the GPS markers. "According to the GPS, we're about thirty minutes away from Mouse's home now. Shall we do a drive-by, do a recon, take a close look around, snap some pictures to see what kind of an area we're looking at, then go find food while we discuss what we found?"

"Yeah, that's a good idea. We did check Google maps. It's not a great area of town, and that might be enough for somebody who's not doing the in-depth work we're doing. But, if I get a chance, I always want to see the locations first."

"Exactly."

They drove through the city, weaving in and out of traffic, following the voice on the GPS. Laszlo laughed at the sexy female tone. Most of the time it was right, but sometimes it was so far off it was ridiculous. He might be out of active duty, but he certainly wasn't out of active life. And right now they needed to combine all their skills—past, present and the ones they had yet to learn—to bring this case to a close. It was the only way they could all move forward.

"I still have trouble believing it's Mouse," Geir stated. "Like you said, there are a lot of other reasons for somebody to hate us. But, after discussing it with everyone, I think it's odd that none of us really knew who Mouse was. Not on the inside. He was always telling stories, making up facts to suit his version of the truth."

"True enough," Laszlo admitted. "It's a little hard to understand why. I mean, I was born in one house, raised in another house, and they can both be confirmed. I never dreamed of making up stories about my family or about where I went to school and did my training."

"Because you were okay with all that. Mouse wasn't. I think the only reason somebody makes up stories is so they can ignore the truth or because they think it's not exciting enough, and they're desperate to be somebody they aren't."

"And maybe Mouse was doing that. So why did he join the navy? Why did he end up a SEAL, like us? The fact that he passed is huge. And yet being a US Navy SEAL doesn't seem to be who he was."

"Honestly I often wondered if he just did it to prove he was capable. That he was strong enough, male enough."

"As in, maybe not having completely accepted his sexuality?"

"Or didn't want the sexuality to change the fact he was male. He was never somebody with a gender-identity issue, I don't think. It was more a case of, he preferred men for his romantic liaisons, but he also preferred men as strictly friends."

"Interesting. Do you think he was a woman-hater?" Laszlo asked, rolling that concept around in his mind. "I never considered that."

"I think it's something we shouldn't dismiss. Yet we

never saw any evidence of that. He was never rude or ugly to women. His language was joking but polite."

"That could then potentially mean our killer is a woman?" That was almost shocking to Laszlo. "There are certainly a lot of women haters out there, but very few killers are women and rarely a killer who operates alone. Women are sometimes paired up with a killer or, for whatever twisted reasons, joined the male in his killing spree, but few women go out of their way to kill multiple people. Definitely the Black Widows are an exception. But those circumstances were motivated by greed. Those women killed off husbands one at a time to inherit whatever they left behind. Consider Aileen Wuornos's case, a serial killer in Florida who killed many of her johns, probably more out of hate for the position she was in than that they were using her services."

"I hadn't considered that," Geir said. "I know very few women capable of such a thing. But that's not to say it doesn't happen. There are many military units where women are as good as the men and as dangerous as the men, serving as snipers, killing machines in female bodies. And, in our situation, it doesn't take a ton of skill to ram a vehicle and kill the occupants."

"Do you think somebody might have been spurned by Mouse? An ex-lover? Someone who loved him but who he didn't love back?"

"I don't think someone could hate him enough to kill the rest of the men in his unit," Geir said quietly. "Honestly I think it'll be somebody who knows all of us and hates us all equally."

"Somebody from the military, from the navy, from another mission, our team, other teams?"

"I'll say, our side. Of course that's not what anybody

wants to hear. Also it'll be somebody who knows us. So again probably somebody from the US military. Whether that means the navy overall, or another SEALs unit, the army, the marines, I don't know for sure. Active or no longer active? Who knows? Unfortunately tens of thousands of trained personnel are quite capable of doing what was done to us. It was mostly strategy, if you think about it."

"The more I think about that, a woman is a valid possibility. And she's employing hit *men* who were hired in multiple cases. Maybe all," he admitted. "Whoever is behind this has used men to do the dirty work." He glanced at Geir to see what he thought about that.

Geir nodded. He had a big tablet in his lap. He was busy flicking through screens with his good hand. "That's a good point. If this person hasn't done any hands-on killing, then we should consider the fact that they weren't capable of it in terms of physical strength or weren't capable of it at an emotional level or plain didn't want to get their hands dirty. Which could be male or female."

"Or it could be someone just distancing themselves from each crime. Removing themselves from the suspect pool." Laszlo shook his head. "Instead of fine-tuning and clarifying the issue," Laszlo complained, "it's getting worse."

Geir chuckled. "What we don't want to do is so finitely narrow down the suspect pool that we toss out our killer."

"But we can't operate on the basis of tens of thousands of suspects either," Laszlo reminded him. "We have to start somewhere."

"Indeed, we do."

"And that's why we're less than a minute away from Mouse's home where he grew up."

MINX WATCHED THE truck slow down and drive past the houses on the block from the shadows of a front porch across the street. Two men were inside the truck, both studying the area until they came to Mouse's house. Anybody who ever came to that house deserved a second look. The men drove past and pulled into the space between two old battered-up cars and just sat there. At least they were smart enough to not get out.

There would be no vehicle left when they came back if they left it here for too long. The gangs in the area were proud of the fact they could take the wheels off any vehicle in less than twelve minutes flat.

At one point they'd been successful in taking out all the streetlamps too.

And then they decided the fire hydrants should be seized up. If there was nothing else, these teens were into bad, useless, antagonistic mischief that caused no end of stress for everybody else. She would love it if somebody would put them away, but their crimes were never bad enough for anybody to focus on them. They hadn't murdered anybody, hadn't shot anybody. The fact that they were increasingly aggravating was definitely cause for concern, but she doubted anybody else gave a shit. She was a counselor and came from this area originally. She knew firsthand on multiple levels.

She had been transferred as a punishment to the local office, one she had no plans remaining at. It was supposed to be temporary, but she suspected her bosses were trying to keep her here. In which case, she would walk. She'd spent enough of her life here. Yes, these kids could use her help. But once anybody found out who she was, they wouldn't listen. She would be respected for having gotten out but also hated for having gotten out.

It was definitely a no-win situation. She didn't have a rapport with any of the locals anymore. She had no kinship, no connection to draw on. And the people here were definitely down and out. But counselors could only work with those who wanted to change—those with a spark of something that said there was another life. She'd often thought she should write a self-help book and go on Oprah, but that seemed so far-fetched, considering where she'd come from, that it put a smile on her face. Mouse had told her that she should do that.

Minx and Mouse had been best friends. For a long time. She was forever putting peroxide over his open wounds and patching them up the best she could. If his mother had ever found out, she would have come after Minx herself. Until one day Mouse had given her a hug and said, "I can't stay." And she'd watched him walk. He'd only been sixteen, already battered and beaten. She lost track of him after that. She tried once to ask his mom about him, only his mom had cheered and said, "He's gone. Likely dead by now. That little freak probably sucked the wrong dick and got his throat cut."

After that, Minx had kept her thoughts to herself. Mouse had had a pretty tough childhood, but he seemed to take most of it in stride. She didn't know how mixed-up he was on the inside because he always presented a decent front for her, even though she had tried to get him to talk about it. But he just shook his head and said she was too young and to not worry about it. He'd figure it out.

Young meant two years younger than him. And when Minx's mom had been busy doing drugs in the back room, his mom had been busy whaling on him for not being man enough to handle whatever it was she wanted him to handle.

Mouse was homosexual, and, at the time, before he left, he was pretty excited about it. He had been conflicted for years only to finally find love in unlikely places. By the time he had a steady boyfriend, he was feeling solid about his choices. His first sexual encounter, not consensual, was at the age of twelve, with one of Mouse's mom's boyfriends. But, instead of turning him off, it had turned him on, as if he'd finally found a whole new world he hadn't known about.

That boyfriend hadn't stuck around, but there had been an interesting change in Mouse. She understood, even though he didn't want to talk about it. And she was fine with that. He did tell her at one time she should try it herself.

She'd chuckled and said she was happy to try men. She just wasn't interested in trying women.

She caught movement in her peripheral vision.

One of the men parked at Mouse's house was getting out of the truck, his gait stiff. He reached up and stretched his arms and shoulders, walking around, kicking out his legs. She frowned as she studied him. He had dark hair and was big, tall, held himself with a stance that said power was in that frame. But more than that, it was the look on his face. Dark, broody ... dangerous, as if he didn't miss much. This was not a man to trifle with.

He turned to look at her. His gaze seemed to see right through her. Yet there was something compelling about his actions, that direct gaze ... the smooth body language as he had walked through life.

Instinctively she stepped back—but knew there was no hiding from that man.

Who the hell was he?

CHAPTER 2

MINX STEPPED BACK slightly, behind one of the porch posts, only enough to be out of their view but still able to keep them in hers. Another trick she'd learned while young.

She shook her head at the memories. They were worse now that she was back in the neighborhood, in sight of her childhood home. Such a misnomer. She stomped back the memories most of the time, but now it was as if they were just a cauldron waiting to boil over. Her childhood had been easier than Mouse's, but it still had sucked. She'd left as soon as she could too. Once Mouse was gone, there didn't seem to be any point in hanging around. But she still had to finish school and to figure out what she would do afterward. In order to do that she had to get away. She had gone back to Maine, after contacting her uncle, asking if there was any way she could come and live with him while she went to school.

"Poor Mouse," she whispered, her gaze on the men who were still walking the block. She hadn't seen many men like that. Not Mouse, not her uncle. Immediately her mind whipped back to her childhood. Thank heavens her uncle had been there for her. He hadn't had a clue what her home life had been like. The minute he knew, he'd paid for her bus ticket. It was the longest trip of her life. But she'd made it, and he'd been the kindest and the most generous soul she'd ever had the good fortune to meet. He'd not only given her a place to live, he'd found her a job and paid for her college. After that she'd gotten scholarships and completed grad school.

When she went into counseling, he'd been thrilled for her—figuring how she'd come from such a rough beginning that she'd be the best person to turn around and help others get out. The trouble was, it was hard to deal with the system, not only the governmental entities involved but the mind-set of the families living here for generation after generation. When people in need were forever ground into the dirt, it was almost impossible to help them reach a place too high for them to envision. Even though it was just normal daily living for many. But Minx understood. She'd been there.

Her gaze slipped back to the men.

The second man, if anything, appeared frustrated, angry. She didn't know if his expression always looked like a thundercloud ready to erupt, but it certainly did at the moment. She sidled slightly closer. She really had no business on this property, but it was deserted and empty. She'd come to check an address on file, but, of course, they'd already booked it. The good thing was, they hadn't taken the children this time. They'd left them with a neighbor. She was waiting for calls to determine where the children would end up—temporary placements. Hopefully keeping the siblings all together and hopefully not placed with a family who beat them and left drugs on the table for them to clean off whenever they felt like it. There was nothing worse than watching two-year-olds having access to drugs guaranteed to ruin their life before it ever started.

This address happened to be right beside her old childhood home.

The men crossed the road and walked down the block past Mouse's house again. It was obvious they cared about only one house. They did stop farther down and looked across the street, studying a couple other houses. She let her gaze follow them, drift over to the house they were studying, but she didn't believe for a moment they cared. They weren't from this neighborhood. They weren't from any neighborhood around here, from what she could see. Both were well-dressed, both fit. Cops? She twisted her face up as she thought about it and then discarded the concept. "So not," she said quietly.

But there was just something about them that had that look of *officialness*. Maybe undercover detectives? But even that didn't seem right. They walked down the block, turned around and came back up on the same side they had parked on. Their gaze wandering every once in a while. They pointed at something as if they were out for a casual walk.

She noted old Nanny sitting on her rocker, watching them too. Nanny was in the corner house, and she didn't miss anything in this neighborhood. She had to be ninety, at least. She also wasn't the kind to let anybody know nothing. She kept her mouth shut. In fact, it was impossible to get her to say anything. Everyone left her alone.

It was probably why she'd lived so long. The two newcomers passed Nanny's place, neither appearing to notice her sitting there rocking away. Nor did Nanny call out. She just studied them suspiciously. Kind of like what Minx was doing herself.

They came back toward the truck, passed it, walked to the other end of the block, crossed the street and came back down again. And she knew they were coming to her. She didn't know how she knew, but years on the streets had fine-tuned her reflexes and intuition. She was one of the few who hadn't been sexually assaulted during her years growing up here. That was because she was fast with a knife, and she made sure she was nowhere to be found when the creepy-crawlers came hunting.

She stepped into the open, leaned on the fence, her arms crossed. She didn't know if they'd be able to see who she was as she had seen who they were. She was dressed in jeans with frayed edges and shoes that had seen better days. Her T-shirt was too large and stained. Her hair was in a chestnut-colored messy bun in the back. She deliberately didn't wear any makeup. That way she fit into the neighborhood, made people a little more apt to answer her questions.

She eyed them with as suspicious a look as was possible. When they approached, she took several steps back. The men slowed their steps and smiled at her. She just glared back.

The one who had been driving stopped and said, "We mean you no harm. We just wanted to ask some questions about your neighbors." He turned and motioned—as she'd figured—at Mouse's old house.

She raised an eyebrow. What did they want with Mouse? "Nobody lives there."

"For how long?"

She shrugged. "The old lady died a while ago."

"No other family?"

So they *were* after Mouse. What had he gone and done with himself? She shook her head. "No, no one else there."

"Where did the rest of the family move to?" the second man asked.

She shifted her gaze to him suspiciously. "No idea."

They studied her for a long moment and then nodded. "Well, if you see Mouse, tell him some friends are looking for him," he said.

She snorted. "Mouse hasn't lived here in well over ten years."

"We know. But we haven't seen him in a while and wondered if he had any connection to his hometown anymore."

"I don't know what the hell you think you're up to, but there's no way in hell Mouse had friends like you."

The men stared at her. The first one said, "Maybe Mouse has changed."

She snorted again. "And maybe you're cops."

The men shook their heads. "That we're not. What we really wanted was to find some of Mouse's family and talk to them."

"Why?"

They hesitated.

She snapped, "If you're not telling me the truth, then don't bother spinning me a tale."

"No, we didn't tell you the truth before. Although we are Mouse's friends," the first man said, his voice hard, and yet there was sadness in it. "Mouse is dead. And we were hoping to be able to tell his family."

"What?" She stared at them. "I don't believe you." She glanced back at the house where Mouse had lived. "His mom passed away months ago, if not longer. She never mentioned it."

"I'm not sure she knew," the first man said. He held out a hand. "I'm Laszlo. Mouse was part of my unit in the navy."

She dropped her hand before shaking his. "Now I know you're lying. Mouse hated water. He'd never have signed up for the navy." Then she frowned. "I know it was a dream of his, but it's not one I thought he'd ever achieve," she muttered, puzzled. "He really was terrified of water."

LASZLO FELT A bolt through his gut that said something here was very wrong. They'd contemplated how to approach her while walking, but he'd noted her statement to be the truth almost immediately. Yet she was suspicious enough of them to have lied. But she knew Mouse, and that was huge. "Sorry?"

"Mouse," the woman said, speaking very clearly and slowly, "was terrified of water."

The two men stared at her. "Are we talking about the same Mouse?" Geir asked.

Laszlo shot him a glance, then looked back at the woman in front of them. She was a mix of contradictions. She was dressed like she fit the area, but she was clean, her eyes had a sparkle, the whites of her eyes shone with health and vitality. He didn't know what she was doing here, but no way she lived here. It all added up to an intriguing package. Not to mention sexy.

He motioned to the house. "Tall, slim, lean, brownish hair?"

"Yeah, that's Mouse. The only son of Gladys next door."

"What was his name? He was Ryan Hanson to us."

She looked at him with a smirk. "Mickey Mouse O'Connor," she said with emphasis on each name. "His mother's idea of a joke. The Mickey part he couldn't stand, and, if anybody knew he was named *Mickey Mouse*, his life would have been over. Especially here. As soon as he could, he took the name Mouse, and that was it. Call him Mickey, and he'd take you down."

"Wow, nice mom," Laszlo said.

The woman in front of them shook her head. "Not. She was a bitch through and through. Nobody here will miss her."

"Did she have any relationship with Mouse?"

She shrugged. "No idea. I haven't seen him since he was sixteen, when he walked away after telling me goodbye."

"But you were close to him back then, weren't you?" He had heard a note of sorrow in her voice.

She nodded, the motion sending curly tendrils of hair flying. "It was hard to say goodbye, but at least he was away from here. She was the most abusive, vindictive woman I've ever met."

"How bad?" Geir asked, his voice hard. "Did she beat him?"

"All the time. Beat him, burnt him, wailed on him, starved him, choked him. It depended on how drunk she was that day, whether her latest boyfriend had broken up with her or not." She shook her head. "What would have been one of the worst things for most guys, ended up being one of the most freeing things in his life. No, I certainly don't excuse the man who molested Mouse. Right or wrong, according to Mouse, that relationship helped him sort out his sexuality."

"Mouse appeared to be fairly well adjusted to being homosexual," Laszlo said.

She glanced at him in surprise. "You knew?"

He nodded. "We all did. It was fine with us."

She continued to stare at him.

He tilted his head to the side. "That bothers you?"

"I'm trying to figure out if I believe you," she said shortly. "You're very much macho males. He had little luck with
strong men accepting him for who he was."

"Strong men wouldn't feel threatened," Geir said with a
dark overtone. "Only men who are afraid of their own
sexuality have trouble accepting others."

Her eyebrows shot up, and she studied the two of them
with interest. "He was really in the navy with you two?"

Laszlo nodded. "We were part of an eight-man unit. He
was with us for a year."

"How did he die?" Her stance relaxed, her anger easing.

"Our vehicle was blown up," Geir said. He shook his
head. "It happened so fast that I don't think he knew
anything hit him."

"He was killed, and you weren't?"

Laszlo shook his head. "No, we weren't. But we didn't
get off easy."

"Neither did Mouse," she said stiffly as if struggling to
come to terms with the news.

They nodded. "We'd have done anything to get him
back. But it wasn't to be. Neither of us could attend his
funeral. We were still in the hospital. It was touch-and-go if
we'd live. I wonder if his mom knew."

"She never said anything to me. Maybe not to anyone."

"She should have known. The military would have informed her," Geir said. "But, if she had no love for him,
maybe all she cared about was knowing where he ended up.
He did get a military burial."

"I didn't know," she said, her voice softening.

Something in her tone had Laszlo looking at her sharply.
"Would you have gone?"

She nodded. "I would have. I knew him well as a boy

and as a young man coming into himself. I was here around the time Mouse and Poppy, the only name I knew the molester by, came together. I remember the joy in Mouse's face when he later found his first real boyfriend, and he felt like somebody cared for the first time. That he wasn't a freak of nature and that maybe, just maybe, he would make something out of his life after all."

"Any idea who his boyfriend was?"

She thought back. "I remember his first name was Lance. The two left town together I believe."

"I know it's not a question you want me to ask, but I have to, just to know. This guy wasn't a john, was he?"

It took her a moment to understand, and then she shook her head. "No. To the best of my knowledge, Mouse never entered the sex trade."

"Would you know?"

Her mouth opened as if to say, yes, then it snapped shut. "No, maybe I wouldn't. He kept telling me that I was too young to understand. At the time I was angry at him for dismissing me so easily. We'd been friends for a long time. But I do understand he changed after he found his first true boyfriend. He looked happy and smiled a lot more. He was more relaxed. He tolerated his mother's fits more."

"Did she still hit him after that?" He watched as she tilted her head, casting her mind back into the past.

"You know, I'm not so sure she did. He was almost fifteen, growing very tall. His mom was not that big. At some point it was beyond her ability to hurt him physically. He always said he wanted to kill her but that her better punishment would be to live long and suffer more." She smiled a bit. "Mouse was a really good kid. But she had twisted him in some ways that it's hard to imagine how it manifested inside."

"Did you see him again after he left?"

She shook her head. "No. I always wanted to. I always wanted to catch up with him and see how he was doing, what he was doing. But he never contacted me. I was probably part of the life he wanted to leave behind. That's the problem with being childhood friends. When people leave, they leave the best and the worst behind."

"And you? Did you never leave?" Laszlo asked.

She just gave him a blank stare.

He tried again. "Has anybody lived in the house since the mother died?"

She shook her head. "Vandals come and go."

"Do you think anybody would mind if we walked through?"

She shrugged. "I don't know who even owns it anymore. Probably the city, along with half a dozen other destroyed homes in this area. The vandals took anything of value a long time ago. By the same measure you shouldn't leave your truck here for too long or it will be stripped."

The two men nodded.

"Thank you for speaking with us," Laszlo said. He walked past her and up the sidewalk of Mouse's house. He turned to look behind to see she was following him. "Are you waiting to see if we steal anything?"

"There's nothing in there you'd want to take," she said. "But it occurred to me, I haven't been inside either. And this might not be a bad time to take a walk down memory lane and say goodbye to Mouse."

He held the door open for her. As he walked in, he called out, "Hello, anyone home?" But no reply came. Most of the windows were missing; the doors hung askew. He doubted he'd find anything in this wreck, but that didn't mean he would waste an opportunity to make sure while he was here.

Knowing she watched everything they did, he did a slow scope through the living room. There were still old pictures on the wall but nothing that showed family, nothing that showed a home or where they might have been before or after this. The furniture was beyond decrepit and stained. There was a coffee table with two storage areas at each end. He bent down and opened each cupboard to check what was inside, only to find them empty. He wandered the room but didn't find anything personal, nothing that pertained to Mouse.

He headed to the dining room next. There was an old cabinet. The surface was scarred and chewed up, as if somebody had used it for woodworking. Laszlo bent, checked the interior of those cupboards and kept going.

When he reached the kitchen, he stopped. Several of the cupboards hung askew. "How much of this damage happened after she was dead?" he asked no one in particular.

"I think those cupboard doors used to fall off all the time," she said. "I remember once, when they fell, she blamed Mouse. And she beat him pretty good for it."

The two men went through all the cupboards, checking for anything that would jump out at them as being important.

"For a friend you're awfully curious about what's in every corner of his house," she said, suspicion in her voice.

Laszlo nodded. "We're looking for anything that would explain some mysteries about his life."

"What mysteries?"

He glanced at her and smiled. "Well, you're one of

them."

"What are you talking about?" she asked.

"It's obvious you don't belong here. I'm trying to figure out why you're slumming for the day." He turned and planted his hands on his hips and stared at her. "Care to share?"

She shoved her jaw out at him. Somehow the pugnacious look appealed to him. That just meant there was something *definitely* wrong with him.

CHAPTER 3

MINX STARED AT him. How had he figured that out? She pinched her lips together. "I don't know what you're talking about."

"Right there, that's a lie," the one man said. "You're just as suspicious of me as I am of you."

She glared at him.

He shrugged and turned back to doing what he was doing. But it looked like they were already done in the kitchen. The accident explained his single black glove ... and potentially the gait she noticed at various times. As if he were stiff and sore. She had meant what she'd said about the accident being hard on Mouse—he'd died after all—but obviously these men had paid dearly as well.

There wasn't much else to the downstairs—a hall closet and a front closet. She watched as they inspected both of those. She was trying to figure out what was going on. Unless there was something suspicious about Mouse's life or death, there was really no reason for this in-depth look into his childhood.

It was painful for her too. She didn't want to remember all the times she'd held him in her arms while he had cried. How many times she'd cleaned up his scratches and wounds and gave him food she'd stolen from her own house. She'd been slightly younger but old in so many ways. And she owed Mouse. He'd saved her when no one else would.

At the same time, she hadn't done anything to find him after he had left. He had crossed her mind many times, but she had never gone looking. Why was that?

Probably because she was afraid of what she would find. She didn't want to know he had died of an overdose somewhere or had been hit with a sexually transmitted disease and then died wasting away in a hospital bed all alone. So many things were wrong with his childhood that she knew could make a serious impact on the type of man he became later. She'd certainly studied enough personality disorders, personality traits and psychological issues people had from child abuse.

But, for some reason, she hadn't allowed herself to find out what had happened to Mouse. Inside, a part of her was still that young girl looking at him as he left the life he had and being so proud because he did leave. Being so hopeful his life would turn out to be that fairy tale she wanted it to be for him. And yet, she must have known inside it wouldn't happen. "I'm a counselor," she said abruptly.

Laszlo, about to step upstairs, stopped and looked at her. "Were you Mouse's counselor?"

She shook her head. "No way. I'm younger than him— than he would be—and I told you how I haven't seen him since he left. Mouse and I were childhood friends. This is his house. The deserted one beside it"—she turned and pointed to the dilapidated building beside them—"was mine."

"So why are you back here, dressed like you should belong?"

"I was transferred to this area. They wanted me to do more outreach in the neighborhood. I was struggling with the whole concept. I came from here—it's not where I wanted to return to." She saw no judgment in Laszlo's eyes.

"Why would they want to send you back here?"

"I think to get me to quit," she said honestly. There was a certain amount of relief in telling somebody. Particularly when that person didn't know anything about the situation.

"Why would they want to do that?" The second man stepped up beside Laszlo.

She studied him a moment. "What's your name?"

"Geir. And this is Laszlo."

She frowned. "Like the mechanical *gear*?"

He shook his head. "It's a Ukrainian version. G-E-I-R."

She nodded. "Interesting. I'm Minx. Minx Montgomery."

"That's an unusual name too."

She nodded. "It is. But then our mothers were not exactly the staid upstanding citizens of the world. Mine was more interested in drugs than beating on me."

"Is she still alive?"

Minx shook her head. "She died of an overdose seven years ago."

"Were you still here?"

She snorted. "No, I did the same thing as Mouse. As soon as I could, I booked it. In my case, I contacted an uncle." She glanced down at her shoes and smiled. "It was the best decision I ever made."

"Your uncle was a good guy?"

"He *is* a good guy," she corrected. "And the only family I stay in touch with."

"Did he have any idea what your life was like?"

"No, he'd lost track of his sister a long time before. People pick and choose who they want to stay in touch with. My mom and I didn't make the grade."

"You mean you and your uncle didn't make the grade," Laszlo corrected.

She chuckled. "Very true. My mother was a very unhappy soul."

"And why are you back here then?"

"Because I did keep track of another friend," she said. "She wanted me to move closer. So I did. But that didn't work out. I moved out within a couple months to the other side of Dallas and worked at a private school, then moved on soon afterward to working for a counseling service connected to the city foster care system. I've been in the same job for five years now. But then I got into trouble with my bosses and got transferred to this division, as they decided I needed to reconnect with the streets. Aka I got shunted to the less desirable location for making trouble."

"Do they know your history?"

"They might, plus this is a tough area, and they can't get anyone to stay in this division. It takes someone with a lot of acceptance and patience," she admitted.

"Why?" Geir asked.

There was something about the taciturn man in front of her. He was very direct with his questions. Normally she'd have found him off-putting, but she liked him.

"Because my boss was harassing me. He wanted sexual favors in order to keep my job. He thought I should stay late and let him have his way with me because he said so." Her voice contained disgust. "Pardon the crudeness, but there's just something about that type of asshole that brings out the worst in me."

"Did you go to the cops?"

"Not then. And my supervisor told me to stay quiet. Said my boss was sorry and not responsible for his actions. I went above that supervisor, and so my supervisor got in trouble, and the guy who was sexually harassing me got a rap on his fingers. Next thing I knew, I was getting a transfer. It was either take it or quit. Obviously I took it."

"And?" Laszlo asked, a look in his eye that said he'd already caught on.

She shrugged. "And then a few days ago I called the cops."

He nodded. "Good girl."

She sneered. "I haven't been a girl for a long time."

"Nope, and that wasn't meant to be sexist, but it was the right thing to do. And I'm glad you did it."

"Why? I'm not sure it was. But I was feeling so stuck."

"No, you're not stuck. It's your choice. You can stay. You can leave. You can move to another city. You can move to another state. I don't know where your uncle lives, but you can always go back where you have somebody who cares."

"It's one of the things I was thinking about as I stood here, watching you park your truck. At first I thought you were cops. But I figured something else was going on. You really don't have that cop look to you."

They both stared back at her, their faces bland.

"What are you? Naval inspectors or detectives or whatever the hell they're called? NCIS, is that it?"

"No, we aren't. Mouse was a friend of ours, and there's a mystery in his life that needs to be solved. So we're trying to do him a solid and figure it out." At that the men clammed up.

She sighed. "And that's all I get to know, is that it?"

"That's it," Laszlo said cheerfully. "And what about you? You just going to stand here beside your mom's old house and watch the world, trying to figure out where you fit in now?"

"I'm trying to figure out what to do now that I'm pretty much persona non grata since I went to the police."

"That figures. So maybe you do need to change states."

"Still have to have references," she said quietly. "Although some parts of the world have a bigger need for my type of skills than others."

"What about your friend you came here to stay with?"

She shook her head. "She isn't the same person anymore."

"Sounds like a story is there in itself," Laszlo said.

She nodded. "There is, but it's not any more pleasant."

"Care to share?"

"No, I don't. If you're not sharing, I'm not sharing."

"Good enough." At that Laszlo ran lightly up the stairs to the second story.

She followed. As soon as they opened the first door, Laszlo pinched his nose. "Time has not taken the smell from in here."

They could see the soiled bedding that had seen much better days. The ceiling held more moldy stains than white surface.

"Wow, this is pretty bad," she said.

"If it was good, it wouldn't still be here," Geir said. "And even a bed or mattress in that kind of shape would have been stolen a long time ago if there wasn't something else going on here."

"She died of alcohol poisoning but wasn't found for several days," Minx said. "That's what you're probably smelling, although I didn't think body odors stuck around that long."

"It tends to permeate everything—mattress, bedding,

walls, ceiling."

They stepped back out of the room and closed the door. There was only one other bedroom. Laszlo walked toward it, and Minx said, "That was Mouse's."

He nodded and opened the door, stepping inside. Geir followed.

Hesitating, but not knowing why, she trailed behind them.

The room was small, only a mattress on the floor, a blanket that was torn, old, crumpled in a corner. They explored the otherwise bare room, stopping to look at the writing on the walls.

She came up behind them. "Maximum pain," she read out loud. "That was Mouse's motto. *Maximum pain.*"

The two men turned to look at her. "Why?"

"Because his mom would always hit him at special points that would give him maximum pain. She'd take out his funny bone. She'd burn him along his nerve endings. She'd place his hand on a hot stove, and, when it was barely healed, she'd do it all over again for maximum pain."

The two men stared at each other, their gazes hard.

Obviously something was going on. She asked, "Does that have meaning for you?"

"You have no idea."

LASZLO STARED AT Geir, both of their minds clicking on the phrase. Mouse had used that phrase a lot when they were working out. As if it was a matter of pride. Laszlo tore his gaze away from Geir's and studied the wall. He pulled out his phone and took picture. Then he wandered around and studied more of the writings, taking several more pictures.

It still didn't give them a clue as to who was doing this to them. But obviously it was someone close to Mouse. Laszlo didn't expect the room to even have this much left after all these years. The needles on the floor now probably meant a couple junkies had stayed for a night or two recently.

Nothing looked fresh. A layer of dust coated everything. ... He wandered round, taking photos of the entire room and then opened the closet door. It was small with shelves on one side. A light bulb with a chain hung from the ceiling. He pulled it, but nothing happened. He turned on the flashlight app on his phone and studied the small space. There was just barely enough room for any young boy's belongings to fit, and that was only if they were perfectly neat and tidy. Most kids didn't fit that category.

Something was stuck far in the back. He reached for it and pulled out a small plastic emblem. It was a replica of the SEALs logo. He shook his head and handed it to Geir. "Maybe even way back then he wanted to be part of that group."

"He always wanted to be a SEAL," Minx said. "That was his thing. He figured, if he could do that, he would be the best of the best." Minx stood behind them. "But I'm not kidding about him having a huge issue with water."

The two men kept looking at the logo.

"A lot of people believe the SEALs are the best of the best," Laszlo said quietly. "But to get there is pretty rough."

"See? That's one of the things about Mouse. He had incredible determination. Incredible focus. But he wasn't necessarily very good at a lot of things. He was always good enough to get through. But he rarely could stick to it afterward. In school even, I helped him with his math, and I was two years behind. But he was always very good at strategy. We played a lot of hide-and-seek. And, while I would just be looking for a place to hide, he would be marking off mentally all the places in the past I'd gone and calculating which was the most likely I'd go to now. In most cases he'd find me instantly. He was always working out the details, planning the angles." She smiled. "I hope he was happy the last few years of his life."

"He was," Laszlo said. "At least as far as we can figure."

"You saw him every day, right?"

"Almost every day. Except for our various leaves, yes. He was a mix of young and old. Full of life, seriously bad jokes," Geir said.

"And stories. He always made up stories."

Laszlo spun around and peered at her. "Did he do that when you were younger?"

She nodded. "He always made up stories about what he would do when he was an adult, when he could get away. He always wanted to be a big shot. He always wanted to have money, lots and lots of money. He figured, if he was wealthy and a big shot, nobody would do to him what his mom had done to him. He figured it was all about power."

"Was he a team player?"

She looked at him with a frown. "Isn't that a question you should be able to answer?"

"When he was younger, was he a team player?" Laszlo rephrased the question. "This is all about his childhood."

She shook her head. "No, he was a loner. And it was always about him. It's one of the reasons I was so heartbroken when he left. I figured the bond we had would be enough. But, instead, it was still all about him. I'd have cheerfully left with him. He refused to take me. Then he had Lance with him—he didn't need me."

"But he couldn't do that to you. You had a mom. You were also much younger."

"And yet I was just as much of an adult as he was. We both had had rough lives. We both had to hide from the men out there." Her voice was caustic. "We both had to worry about the drugs and the booze and the fight for food. And mostly, after nightfall, we'd bundle up together to stay warm outside. Because our mothers had visitors."

CHAPTER 4

THE MEN STARED at her for a long moment, and she watched a muscle flicker in Laszlo's jaw. Her words had disturbed him in a big way. Interesting. So many wouldn't care.

"Were you ever assaulted?"

She shook her head. "Several tried. I became very good at slashing back with a knife. Even now I don't go far without one." Her smile was wry. "I was tempted to use it on the bloody boss in the office. But it wouldn't have been his face that I would've cut."

The men grinned appreciatively.

"The trouble is, it's easy to get soft when you're away from this environment," Geir said. "So even though, in your mind, you're capable and ready to handle whatever, it's not so simple."

She nodded. "I know. It's one of the reasons I watched you two so carefully. One never really knows who the enemy is. It's often one of the closest in your circle, and you didn't even see him coming."

She watched as the two men looked around and then started toward the stairs. "There was a secret hiding place," she said.

The two men stopped and looked at her. "Where?"

"Tree house in the back," she said quietly. "We spent a

lot of time up there." She brushed past them and led the way to the kitchen door and onto the creaky porch. She stepped carefully as floorboards were already missing, and it looked like some critter had taken up residence underneath. She led the way to the backyard full of heavy overgrown oak trees. She pointed to the top. "It's up there."

"How did you get up?"

She laughed. "Like this." She raced around to the side of the tree and started to climb. She wasn't surprised when Laszlo was hot on her trail.

Every step she took brought back even more memories. The two of them laughing, the two of them playing, the two of them crying. The two of them hiding from all the groans and moans and creaks inside the houses. One stealing food, the other dropping a bucket to bring it up so it could be eaten in peace. The weather in Dallas was up and down during winter. Some winters it stayed at seventy-five degrees; other winters it would drop below the freezing point. And they'd learned to bring blankets and pillows and homework if they had to. They tried candles, but there was always the fire issue. So flashlights had become the norm. Mouse had become adept.

She made it to the old hiding place and stepped onto one of the big branches.

Laszlo came up behind her and took one look. "Wow, this is really well hidden." He glanced at her. "Did you guys build it?"

She shook her head. "No, but we added to it. We ended up stealing all the materials from various houses in the neighborhood," she admitted. "Hopefully they didn't need it as much as we did."

There were no furniture or blankets, no personal belongings anymore. But that didn't stop Laszlo from taking photographs and studying marquees they had put on the boards. "Band-Aids?" He pointed to several bandages stuck between the floorboards.

She nodded. "I kept a pretty decent first aid kit for him."

He froze and looked at her. "That bad?"

"Oh, yes, that bad."

He whistled. "Poor Mouse."

"Yes, poor Mouse, but he would have hit you if he'd heard you say that."

"I know. I know. We were trying to figure out where else he might have lived. The guys were all talking, but we recalled different locations. Somebody said he had been in California."

"California would make sense to me," she said. "He always talked about going there. Even when he was little. He wanted to go to Coronado and San Diego. He figured, if he got close enough to the main SEALs base, he could become one somehow. But he and I both knew it wouldn't happen." She chuckled. "In his mind, anything would have been an improvement on what he had been doing here. He was way too young then, wasn't he?"

"Yes, if he was only sixteen." Laszlo thought a moment, took several more photos, tucked the phone in his pocket and said, "Ladies first."

She shrugged, stepped between the two men, noting how small this space was with three adults in the tree house, and slowly made her way back down the tree. As she stood on the ground, waiting for the two men to join her, she realized just how much of her life had been wrapped up with Mouse. Even now the memories were inside, deep inside, but never buried—and never forgotten.

"When he left," she said as Laszlo landed beside her, "I was really devastated. And it never crossed my mind to go after him or to find out where he'd ended up. There was a finality to his goodbye."

"Sometimes you need to let people go. Other times you need to let them go so you can do what you need to do on your own."

"Words of wisdom." She stared at him, wondering at his insight. She hated to say it, but she liked him all the more. "Are you sure *you're* not a counselor?"

He shook his head. "No, but I've spent the last couple years recovering from horrific physical injuries," he said quietly. "And I had to speak with more than a few counselors about my own issues."

She nodded. "I gather you were badly injured when Mouse died?"

"All seven of us were." Laszlo hesitated and looked at her seriously. "It's one of the reasons we're trying to investigate Mouse's life. There are suspicions …"

She stared at him in horror. "What are you talking about? Wasn't it a military accident?"

He nodded. "It was written up as one. That's why it took us so long to figure it out."

Still confused, she shook her head. "I get that I'm missing all the details. But how could somebody have possibly created an accident that would have injured so many of you? Unless it really was an accident. Just a military one."

"We've come to the conclusion it wasn't an accident at all. As far as we're concerned, the blast that blew us up was deliberately set. Which means …"

A small cry escaped. "Please don't tell me that. Please don't tell me Mouse, who had one of the worst childhoods anybody could have had and was so happy to take off to join the navy, could actually have been murdered."

But he just looked at her quietly, sadness, grief, and anger in his gaze. And she knew it was true. Poor lonely Mouse had been murdered.

"You sure as hell better get that asshole," she snapped. "And you keep him away from me. Because otherwise I'll take him out myself."

LASZLO AND GEIR drove out of town and stopped at a hotel. They booked a room, neither of them needing to do the long drive again tonight. Then they headed to the café next door. It looked to be one of the old popular mom-and-pop restaurants that served burgers and fries and not a whole lot else. Laszlo was happy to have a burger. As he sat down, a text came in from his brother. "Jair is stuck eating pasta again tonight." Laszlo grinned. "The new bodyguard/cook I hired to look after my father and brother is a huge pasta fan. I think my brother is sick of it already."

"He's not at the point of being grateful he has a hot meal yet?"

"Not yet apparently. I told the bodyguard, Petro, that Jair wasn't a huge fan, so I think he's punishing him with extra pasta."

Geir snorted. Two cups of coffee arrived in front of them. It was thick, black, almost sludgelike. Laszlo lifted his, took a sip and grinned. "Coffee like they used to make it. Still with the grounds."

The large woman standing in front of them asked, "Burgers?"

There was no menu in her hands, no chalkboard any-where around he could see showing a menu, so he nodded. "Please."

She nodded, turned and walked away.

Laszlo lifted his eyebrows at Geir. "Really old-school."

"And I bet, if we don't like the food, it's a case of *too damn bad*."

Laszlo chuckled. "Maybe I should tell Jair that. He's got to be a little happier about the fact he's getting three meals a day."

"How is that working out for them?"

"We had temporary people in place, waiting on a more permanent solution. Petro is more long-term. Yet it's only been two days now. And two meals of Italian. But then Petro is Italian, so that makes sense."

Laszlo sent his brother a quick message, telling him to enjoy it and to eat it and to be grateful somebody else was cooking it for him and their father. Both needed the extra carbs. He set his phone down beside him, looking up at Geir. "What's your thoughts on Mouse?"

"I'm not sure what to think," Geir said. "We knew his childhood was rough, his body covered in scars, most likely from his mom. That she got away with that all those years just pisses me off." He shook his head. "What really got me was the writing on the wall. *Maximum pain*."

"And that she died so recently also pisses me off," Laszlo added. "I'd like her to have suffered longer."

Geir nodded. "It's a sad scenario. But I don't know that it helps us now."

"That's the problem. So now we have some idea what his childhood was like, but we don't know where he went when he left. Although Minx did confirm California potentially,"

Laszlo added.

"He made his way to Coronado for naval training, didn't he?"

"He did." Laszlo pulled the plastic SEALs pin out of his pocket, keeping it after Geir had looked at it, and placed it on the table. "I didn't even know they made these things. This is like a toy that comes out of a cereal box."

Geir picked it up and studied it. "It's not a true copy. But for somebody who had plans and fantasies of a bigger, better life, I'm sure it was a symbol for him."

"But the thing is, he did make it as a SEAL. He was one of us."

Geir smiled. "He did make it. And of all the things in his life, I'm sure that one of his proudest moments was when he passed BUD/S training and was accepted into the world he so desperately wanted to be in."

"Interesting what Minx said about Mouse being very focused," Laszlo stated, "and yet very poor at so many things because that's what we found too, didn't we? Even though he was one of us, and he had passed all the training, he sucked at so many things."

"I know," Geir said, nodding. "Mouse couldn't navigate worth a damn. Yet he was a tech wizard."

"He couldn't hit his target unless somebody stood right in front of him either. Until we helped," Laszlo said.

"But he was a hell of a driver," Geir added.

"He was. He improved so much, but how much of that was because we made a place for him?" Laszlo asked. "And I don't mean that in a bad way. But it makes me wonder what another unit would have done with him."

Geir nodded. "You're right. None of us cared about his sexuality because we were all comfortable with ours. None of us were intimidated by him. If anything, we felt sorry for him." Geir paused. "Do you think he felt that?"

"I don't know. I imagine sometimes, yes. It became a bit of a joke. He was so handicapped in so many things."

"How many times did we wonder how he made it through training, right?" Geir added.

Laszlo nodded. "That's exactly right. And I still don't know the answer to that. I wonder if he was put into our unit on purpose."

"Absolutely he was. The question is, whether that was to make him want to quit or thinking we would adopt him."

"I wonder if anybody could tell us."

"I don't know whether they could tell us or whether they *would* tell us," Geir said. "Our command was never very clear. We followed orders blindly, remember?"

"Too blindly as we now realize that we drove our vehicle over a mine planted just for us."

"Right." Gear frowned, choked down the word.

The men sat quietly sipping their thick black coffee, contemplating what Mouse's life had been like.

Then the waitress returned with two huge platters with some of the largest burgers Laszlo had ever seen. And they looked superb. He smiled at her and lifted his coffee. "Any more?"

She beamed and hustled away.

He glanced down at the plate and said, "Wow."

Geir nodded. "If this doesn't ruin my gut, I will believe my stomach's healed," he joked.

They picked up the fries still so hot they were almost impossible to bite, which gave them fair warning the burgers would be just as hot.

As they worked their way through the fries, the waitress

returned with the coffeepot and filled their cups. She left again without a word.

The two men chuckled.

"Any idea how much we're paying for this?" Laszlo asked.

Geir shook his head. "I didn't see a sign, did you?"

"No, I didn't." He reached for his burger and picked it up. It was so big it should have been cut in half, but he figured they'd probably toss him out of the restaurant if he did that. With his first bite, he was lost. When he could talk, he said, "It's amazing."

Geir's face lit up. "I was hoping you would say that. I'm really hungry."

The burger was big and juicy. Laszlo tugged off his glove and picked up the burger. He was afraid to put it down in case it would fall apart. Beautiful meat juices dripped down his fingers onto the plate, making a mess of his hand, though he didn't care. He dug into the burger until it was completely gone. He sat back, wiping his hands on a napkin, his stomach full. "I don't think I've ever had such a good burger."

He glanced around the place. A couple other tables were full, those men doing the same thing. They were plowing through these monster burgers with no talking. But then who could talk? It was all they could do to hold up their burgers and stop them from self-destructing in their hands.

His had pickles on it. Normally he wouldn't eat pickles. But they tasted so damn good, he did. There was also some kind of sauce. He wasn't sure, but it might have been a chipotle sauce. Again, not something he would have ordered, but, as part of the package, it was perfect. Happy, he finished off his fries and sat, letting everything digest.

The woman came back, grabbed his plate, looked at him and asked, "Another?"

His eyes rounded as he shook his head. "No, I think I'm good with one."

She gave him a quick nod and left.

His mind was still amazed at the question. "Do you think anybody could eat two of those things?" He glanced at Geir still working on the first half of his, trying to take it easy. Laszlo said, "If you can't finish it, I'll take it over."

Geir nodded. "I'm good as long as I eat slow. Normally my system is stronger than it is at the moment. If I treat it right, it will be back to normal soon."

Laszlo took a break and sipped some coffee. Geir still had a massive pile of fries. "I wonder how many people leave food on the plate here."

"Never twice," Geir admitted. "I don't imagine they take that kindly."

Laszlo chuckled. "Maybe not." He returned to the issue at hand. "How do we find other people who might have known more about where Mouse went?"

"Ask Mason for whatever the military has on file. If that's something he can't do, then we should ask Levi."

Lazlo stole a few of Geir's fries and sent Erick a text, asking him to request Mason get information on Mouse's residence in California and anything else he can find. They would head home first thing in the morning but were quite prepared to head on to California if need be afterward.

Then realizing he didn't remember Mouse mentioning owning his own vehicle, he added a note saying, **Check the DMV database if he owned a vehicle.**

Erick acknowledged with a text as Laszlo watched Geir make his way through the last of the fries. "I'm surprised you're eating as much as you are," he said.

Geir shrugged. "So am I. It's good."

The front door opened, and Laszlo looked up to see Minx walk in. She'd cleaned up some, had a big smile on her face, as if knowing she was with friends. The waitress bustled over and gave her a hug. She had hardly spoken to them, but apparently Minx warranted a personal greeting. The waitress motioned to the front counter, and Minx nodded and took a seat, the two of them in an animated conversation.

As if her instincts had kicked in, she turned around to sweep the room. Her gaze landed on them, and she frowned. She got up and walked over. "What are you two doing here?"

"Having dinner." Laszlo asked lazily, "Is there a law against that?"

She leaned forward. "Mouse used to work here. It's the one job he did have that got him away from his mom. Agnes over there used to feed us anytime we didn't have food that day."

CHAPTER 5

M INX DIDN'T KNOW how she felt about seeing the two men here. The fact that they found this café was amazing. Agnes and Bart had been running it since before anybody could remember, but they never advertised. Outside of a very worn, faded café sign on the front of the building, there was very little to suggest the food here was the best in town. But word of mouth had traveled, and the old-timers were good at not sharing in order to keep it for themselves.

It wasn't very busy at the moment, but Minx had been here at times when there was standing room only as they waited for people to eat and to move out. People were more than happy to wait for well over an hour for a burger here.

Laszlo patted the seat of the booth beside him and said, "Join us."

She raised an eyebrow and considered the issue. "You want to question Agnes, don't you?" Her suspicions were confirmed when she watched him nod.

"Absolutely I do. But that doesn't mean I don't want to have a meal with you."

She motioned at his almost empty plate. "I'd be too late for that."

"I'd have invited you if I'd had your number," he said with a cheerful grin. "We had no idea about this place."

"Tourists never do," she said. "It survives by word of

mouth. And the trouble is, it's often very hard to get a seat in here."

"They've been open a long time, I gather."

"Over thirty years," she said. "Mouse and I used to run here on some particularly rough days. Agnes always had a big smile. If you behaved yourself, stuck to the right side of life, she would support anybody. If you even make an attempt to get your life together, she'd support you any way she could. Screw her over though, and you're done." Minx's tone came out low.

Just then Agnes walked toward them. "I heard my name." She placed a large platter of burger and fries down in front of Minx. Beside it was a bowl of salad. "If I know you, Minx, you haven't been eating properly."

Minx flushed. "Agnes, I'm doing fine."

She shook her head. "Like hell. You were scrawny as a kid, and you're scrawny as a woman. You should never have left."

"That's definitely something I've considered over the years," Minx said with a smile. "You're all heart, Agnes."

She nodded. "I am." She glanced at the two men and asked, "You know Minx?"

There was a hard undertone to her voice, as in, if they messed up, she'd be on them in a heartbeat. But, if they were friends, then she'd be okay to welcome them into her inner circle of accepted patrons.

"To be honest, we only met her today," Laszlo said quietly. "But there's a lot to like," he admitted. "And, no, we're not fly-by-night visitors. We came to check into the history of a friend of ours who's passed away."

Agnes crossed her arms over her ample bosom and stared at him. "Cops?" she barked.

The two men shook their heads.

"We were in the navy. He was one of our unit. He passed away in an accident a couple years ago. An accident where we were all badly injured. Now that we're finally back on our feet, we decided to come and do a memorial trip for our friend."

"Who's your friend?"

Minx stiffened, knowing what would come next. She turned to look at him, looked over at Agnes and decided to do it herself. "Agnes, it's Mouse."

Agnes stared at her in shock, her gaze going from both men back to Minx. "Mouse? He's dead?"

Minx nodded. "According to them, yes."

But then Agnes shook her head. "Oh no. Oh no. You guys got that wrong."

Geir, who'd been quiet up until then, leaned forward. "Why?"

"If you'd said military—army, maybe even air force … I'm not sure about that—but the fact that you said navy … Hell no. Mouse was terrified of water."

The two men exchanged confused glances. Laszlo said slowly, "That just doesn't fit. We haven't seen Mouse afraid of anything."

They glanced at Minx. "Any chance he was just putting on that fear?"

Both Agnes and Minx shook their heads. "No, I don't think so. He was seriously scared of water," Minx said. "We were supposed to take swimming lessons in school. But we couldn't even get him near the water. When he was younger, he would just scream the minute anybody tried to push him in. At one point a bigger bully picked him up and tossed him into the shallow end, and you'd have thought Mouse was drowning, even though he could stand up in the water. It was only midthigh deep. He screamed and screamed like there was no tomorrow."

"Any idea where that came from?"

She hesitated, not really wanting to share or to open up wounds from so long ago.

But Agnes had no problem doing so. "That bitch of a mother. She tried to drown him several times."

"Really?" Geir asked.

"She used to hold him underwater until he almost passed out, and then she'd bring him up again so he could breathe, just to do it again and again."

Minx's voice was low, sad. "He never told us about it until after the fact, like years later. I didn't really believe him or realize just how serious it was until the swimming pool incident. He wouldn't walk along a river. He wouldn't do anything like that." She turned to them again. "Maybe your Mouse isn't my Mouse. Do you have a picture?"

Geir pulled his phone out of his pocket and swiped through images. He frowned, looking for one. "I don't have one," he said. "What about you, Laszlo?"

"I don't know if I have one on my phone. I certainly do on my laptop." He glanced at his truck. "I can grab it."

Geir reached over, his palm up. "Give me the keys. I'll go get it."

Laszlo handed him the keys, and Geir hopped up, walked out of the restaurant and headed to the truck.

Minx couldn't help but see the tight shiny skin and odd-looking fingers on Laszlo's hand. She said nothing but noted the single black glove sitting on the table. At least he'd taken it off to eat.

"Six feet, skinny as a rail, scars all over his body, reddish-brown hair in the sun. Kind of blond sometimes, kind of red at other times."

She jolted at the description. Slowly she said, "Yes, all of that is correct." She glanced over at Agnes. "He really was afraid of water, wasn't he?"

"Yes," she said adamantly. "But I suppose it's possible, as he grew up, he faced his fears?"

"That's a major one though," Minx said. "Still he really wanted to be a Navy SEAL."

"Well, he'd certainly had to overcome his fear of water for that," Laszlo said. "And the Mouse I knew passed the training."

"Do you know how he did in BUD/S training?" Minx asked. She watched him start in response to her question. She shrugged. "I like to read."

His gaze stared at her longer than necessary.

She flushed. "Okay, so I like to read military romance novels," she said irritably.

His gaze warmed with humor.

Irritating and yet … attractive. Damn it. She raised both hands in frustration. "Just answer the question."

"That training is only for SEALs," he admitted. "Some of the navy training he did struggle with. But the thing about Mouse was, he was focused. It seemed like he would get to a certain level where he figured was good enough, and then he'd stop, and he'd tackle something else. But he was smart."

"That's also the way he was. He needed to pass school in order to keep going, but he never did really well. Yet he was incredibly smart. He struggled with so many things in life, but he didn't want to outshine so many people because he figured it would get him unwanted attention."

"I wonder how much of it was a game to him? Or does

he pretend to not be smart to avoid unwanted attention? Or is he really good at some things and not others?" At that Laszlo leaned forward. "Because there were some things he just wasn't all that good at, I thought. It was almost like he was hindered in some way, or maybe it was the abuse growing up, but it seemed like some simple things he couldn't do." He hated to think he'd been conned, but it was possible. "Or was he putting it all on?"

"I've seen that before with very smart people," Minx added. "They're supersmart in one area, and they're almost commonsense stupid in others. On his exams he would answer 100 percent correct on maybe ten questions, but he wouldn't even bother answering five others. He would end up sitting right among the average of the class. He told me about it one time. When I tried to question him, he said, *Life's too dangerous if people know what you can really do.*"

Silence filled the restaurant as if understanding something odd was coming. A big man, almost as big as Agnes, but taller, a big apron around his waist, came out with a towel in his hand. "What's going on?" His voice was just below a bellow.

Agnes turned to him. "This man and his friend came looking into Mouse's history. They think he was one of their own unit who was killed, but we think they have the wrong Mouse."

"Except that the man does fit the same description of our Mouse," Minx said quietly. "Bart, you're looking as healthy as ever."

Bart grinned, showing his missing two front teeth. He patted his overwhelmingly large belly and said, "That's because of Agnes. She takes good care of me." Almost immediately the smile dropped away as he said, "I hope we're talking about a different man. Mouse had a shit life already. He deserved to have something good happen in his life, not an early death."

Just then Geir came back with the laptop. He handed it to Laszlo.

Laszlo quickly booted it up. When it went live, the others stood silently beside him. He shifted through the images he kept on file. As soon as he had a good one of Mouse, he flipped around his laptop so the others could see the photo.

Silence descended.

Minx's voice, choking on tears, whispered, "Yes, that's Mouse."

Agnes nodded as did Bart. "Best damned mixed-up kid I ever had here," Agnes said.

Bart nodded his agreement. "We were here for him as much as we could be. He was always hungry, always starved, his body always trying to heal from whatever recent beating that bitch gave him." He shook his head.

"That's the thing. He ended up in the navy," Agnes emphasized.

Bart's gaze, which had been sharp before, now narrowed to knife points as he stared at the two men. "Navy? Our Mouse?"

Laszlo slowly nodded. "He was one of our unit."

Bart studied him for a long moment. "I don't want to call you a liar, son, but our Mouse wouldn't have gone anywhere close to water." At that he looked down at the plate in front of Minx. "You better eat all that. You're getting skinnier every time I see you." He turned and headed back to the kitchen.

LASZLO DIDN'T KNOW what to think. They'd identified his Mouse was their Mouse, and yet, at the same time, it couldn't possibly be him because of his fear of water. With Agnes now returning behind her counter, Laszlo looked at Minx who was plowing through her burger. "How can Bart possibly eat burgers when he has no front teeth?"

She shook her head. "I wondered that myself. But don't you dare ask him."

"No, wouldn't do that."

She motioned with her head toward the photo as she chewed. "I don't suppose I could have a copy of that, could I? I haven't had a photograph of him since he was sixteen."

Geir straightened, looking at her intently. "If we give you a copy, will you give us a copy of when you knew him?"

She nodded. "Deal."

"Do you have many photos from back then?"

She shook her head. "No. None of us had cell phones or cameras. I think that's the most recent picture I have of him. He gave it to me himself. I think it was from one of those machines that you sit in and take pictures for a dollar. He wanted me to have it before he left."

"We'd really like to see that."

She nodded. "It was years ago, but I scanned it into a photo imagery program, then saved it. So, it's not great in terms of quality, but you'll see the resemblance."

"And you're sure he had no siblings?"

"As sure as we can be," she said. "You can check birth records and any other family tree information. But, as far as I know, his mom only had one child. And that was a damn good thing. Although there was talk of a stepfather when he was little. But he didn't talk about him much, and I never saw such a person."

Laszlo agreed, but it was a conundrum. "He either has a twin brother, or he learned to deal with his fear of water."

"Honestly, from my perspective," she mumbled, her mouth still finishing off a bite of food, "neither works. Because it seems far-fetched he'd have a twin, but it seems equally far-fetched he overcame such a major traumatic episode in his life."

"True, but people have done that."

She nodded. "They do. And, if he did, I'm really proud of him. That he actually made it to where he wanted to be is huge."

The two men looked at each other, and Laszlo realized they were both wondering if they should tell her about Mouse becoming a SEAL and then decided no. He brought up his email program. "What email do you want me to send the photo to?"

She gave him her email address. He attached the photo, and, while she watched, he hit Send. She beamed. "Thank you." She picked up a french fry and popped it into her mouth. Then said, "And do you want me to attach Mouse's picture too?"

"Sure, that would be perfect."

Her fingers clicked through her phone. She lifted her gaze. "Sent."

His phone pinged. He brought up the email and clicked on the attachment. Instantly a young teen's face filled the screen. Laszlo studied it intently. There was a resemblance but not clear enough to be sure. However, there was also a hint of the mark on his neck. Only it wasn't big enough to be sure. It was more of a shadow though. He passed the phone to Geir.

"Did he have a tattoo on his neck and shoulder?" Geir

asked studying the photo before he handed the phone back with a shrug. "It could be our Mouse." He studied her face and reiterated, "Did he?"

She frowned. "He had a birthmark, but it wasn't a tattoo."

But a birthmark might have been tattooed to cover it up. There was just enough resemblance to think they were talking about the same man. To change the subject, he looked at Minx and asked, "Can you eat all that?"

"I haven't eaten all day," she confessed.

"That's not cool," Laszlo said, quickly forwarding the message and attachment to Erick. "You should know better than that."

"I do know better, but I can't say I'm very happy at the moment, so there's a tendency to not give a shit."

"Have the police followed up with you at all about your complaint?"

She nodded. "I'm supposed to go in tomorrow morning and talk to them."

"Good. That will help." Laszlo watched the emotions cross her face. He'd always been sensitive to other people's moods and thoughts. In her case, there wasn't a whole lot of deduction needed. Her face was an open book. She hated her job and was angry at the situation she was in. She wanted justice but didn't believe she would get it. And he could relate to that.

"Not really. I'm afraid I'll just get more repercussions. I've already been shunted into a dead-end job in a dead-end part of town. They can't dock my pay, but I'm sure, if they could find a way, they'll do that too."

"So it's time to move," Laszlo said. "If you're really stuck here, and you've got family and friends here, then stay. But if nothing's holding you here, move and get a fresh start."

"And where do you suggest I move?"

"It's a huge world out there. I can't say any place in particular is better or worse than another."

Geir nodded. "We had that same problem after our accident. We were placed all over the country. But, the thing is, we had been such close friends while we were in the navy that, during our recoveries, keeping track of each other as we progressed, it seemed natural we'd want to be together. Nobody else knew the real challenges we faced. Nobody really understood what it was we had to deal with emotionally and physically, except for each other. So we've slowly been relocating to Santa Fe, New Mexico."

"All seven of you?"

Laszlo nodded. "Four of us are there now, with me trying to find a permanent place. And Geir here has a place but hasn't been living there."

"I probably will now," Geir said. "I just need to take care of a few things first."

"While New Mexico has never been on my list of places to move to," she looked at them, "why did you choose there?"

"Kat," they said together.

Laszlo chuckled at the confusion on her face. "A prosthetic designer and engineer who lives and works there. We keep making trips to see her anyway, so we decided, since Badger, one of our unit, was already there, that would be the easiest to relocate to. Besides, the weather is great. It's a smaller laid-back community, and it suits us."

She nodded. "Nothing really replaces a sense of family or community. I haven't had that in a long time. Maybe since Mouse left," she said sadly. "It was never quite the same afterward."

"Time to build a new one then," Geir said. "That's not easy, which is why we've all decided New Mexico is for us. At least if one has to have surgery or is setting up a business or is moving into a new place, the others can help support us."

"It sounds wonderful." She smiled at them. "You don't realize how alone you are until you see other people who have created a solution for their own lonely life."

"When we were full-active duty," Laszlo said, "we had a lot of friends. The navy is a massive business and family community all at once. When you belong, you really belong. But, when you step back and out of it, it's incredibly difficult to replace that same sensation of belonging to something important."

"And I don't think I've ever had that," she said. "I thought that's what I'd have by going into counseling. But, working for the city, well, let's just say the conditions are ugly. I used to love my job, but now we're all overworked, underpaid, underappreciated, and there's not a real connection with any of the files that come across my desk. And I really wish there was."

"What about going into a different kind of counseling? Like addiction counseling or maybe even family counseling?" Geir asked.

"I have to counsel what I know," she said with a smile. "But not sure I want to deal with that. It hits too close to home."

"If you went into the private sector, you would find a very different response to your work."

She nodded. "And I've thought about it. Particularly since I had to make a decision to do something about my supervisor. If this gets any nastier, I will not be welcome anywhere in the industry here."

"Sexual harassment is not allowed, no matter what industry," Geir said firmly.

She snorted. "I get that you guys are all out there with honor, defending the country and whatnot, but don't forget this is still the US. And sexual harassment goes on everywhere."

"But you've taken the first step to setting your boundaries of what's allowed and what's not allowed. And that will help other people stand up for their rights."

She popped another french fry in her mouth, her gaze again going from one to the other. "You two are living in a world I don't recognize. When you're raised with a drugged-up mother with her multiple boyfriends, and you fight for your own personal space and safety on a daily basis, and your friends are all in a similar boat, *your* world is something we don't even recognize."

"But you did recognize that when you went to your uncle's," Laszlo reminded her. "And you are trying to help other people recognize it through the work you do."

She frowned at him. "How do you know that?" she challenged.

He smiled, loving her spunk. "Because you want to do the right thing. Even though you're not sure sometimes what that is or how to make it happen, you're the kind of person who wants justice." The suspicion in her gaze made his grin widen. "Look at what you did. Somebody sexually harassed you, and, instead of him getting punished through the right channels, he got off scot-free. You're the one who got punished. And that doesn't sit right with you. So, what did you do? You decided to take it a step further and make sure justice happened. Whether you like it or not, you're one of the *good guys*. And whether you believe in yourself or you don't, one of these days you'll wake up and realize that, in order to do work that makes you feel good about yourself and about your own life, you'll have to help others find justice for themselves."

Her jaw dropped as she stared at him.

But he could see awareness slamming into her. "And, no, I'm not a shrink. But I've lived a long time with an amazing amount of people who have a lot of issues. And there's one thing about being two years in recovery. It gives you an awful lot of time to think."

CHAPTER 6

MINX WAS READY to pay her bill and leave. Not that she really wanted to go home to her temporary quarters. She had no intention of staying here. Twenty days into her punishment, she was no more content to be back in her old stomping grounds than she was on her first day. Just as she got up, her phone rang. She glanced at the number, frowned but hit Talk. "Hello?"

No answer.

"Hello? Anyone there?"

Nothing. She shrugged, ended the call and tucked it into her pocket.

"Wrong number?" Laszlo asked.

"Who knows? I've been getting a lot of them lately."

"Any idea why?"

"How the hell would I know?"

"They didn't start after you went to the police, did they?"

She was half standing, ready to leave, but she clunked back down into her seat as his words hit home. She frowned as she stared at him. "I'm not sure."

"When did you go to the cops?"

"A few days ago. I gave them all the details. They would write up the statement, and I'm supposed to go in and sign it. And that'll open the file officially, and they'll do whatever it is the police do."

"Do you think anybody contacted the guy you were having investigated to let him know what you were doing?"

"I imagine they would have to," she said in a reasonable tone. "You can't think these hang-up calls have anything to do with that?" Then she gave him a narrow gaze. "I'm sure it's just a wrong number."

"Sure. That's probably all it is," Laszlo said, but his words didn't match his tone. "But mention it to the cops."

She pulled her phone back out and flicked through her messages. "You guys are trying to scare me."

"No, not at all," Laszlo said. "Maybe alert you to a hidden danger you hadn't considered."

"Such as?" she asked in a challenging voice. "I certainly didn't post it on social media or anything."

"Why not?"

"It's not my way. I figured there would be enough media storm over it all soon enough."

"Exactly. So how do you know somebody from the police station didn't see and/or hear what you were talking about and might have already jumped to that conclusion?"

"It's just as likely they contacted the office where I worked and said I'd been in. The case has already been opened, so maybe they jump-started it already." She shrugged. "It's to be expected."

"Yes, but sometimes things can get ugly, even if we're in the right and other people are in the wrong."

She stared at him for a long moment. "I had a hard time going to the police in the first place. Don't start making me wish I hadn't."

He raised his eyebrows. "That's not what I'm trying to do. I want you to take precautions. And phone calls like this could be just the beginning."

She felt a shiver slide down her back. "Well, that's definitely not confidence-inspiring," she snapped. "And, if this escalates, I'll end up having to quit my job and move anyway."

He nodded. "Do you live alone?"

She narrowed her gaze at him. "Yes. I've been here less than a month. I rented a furnished basement suite. The owners are away on vacation right now, so the upstairs is empty."

The two men exchanged a glance.

She shook her head. "No, no more scare tactics."

Laszlo pulled a notepad from his pocket, ripped off one sheet from it and wrote down his phone number. "If you need us, we're here overnight. Probably leaving in the morning."

She snorted. "There better not be anything happening overnight." But she couldn't stop herself from grabbing his note. She studied the phone number, took his pen and wrote his name down. "If I don't know whose number it is, I'll never dial it."

He didn't say anything but watched as she punched the number into her phone.

"So what kind of stuff am I supposed to watch out for?"

"Being followed, more phone hang ups. Intruders. Stalkers. Males who are anything but friendly and light. Same thing with email. It's not hard to hack websites anymore. If somebody wanted to send an email to you at your work address, that would be easy enough to do as well."

"You guys are just a bundle of love, aren't you?" She hadn't meant her words to come out quite so caustic as they did, but, at the same time, she meant them. "I was raised in the streets. It takes a lot to pull one over on me, but I will admit I haven't been living on that rough edge, worrying about my survival, in quite a while."

He nodded. "Exactly."

Geir spoke up. "Any other weird phone calls? Anybody watching you a little too intently? The sense that somebody was following you? Any nasty gifts? People posting hate posts on your social media pages?"

She stared at them. "You really think that'll happen?"

"We're afraid it could."

She tapped her phone, checking her emails. "This came in this morning. I wasn't even worried about it. I just figured it was spam." She clicked on it, twisted her phone sideways to see it larger and held it out for them.

"Is this your personal email?" Laszlo looked at the address. "Yes, it is. That's the one I sent the photo to." He read it out loud, "*Stop now, bitch.* Well, that's to the point."

"Is it though?" she asked. "I thought it was just spam."

"Maybe. But if it's because of this sexual harassment report, it could get much worse."

Just then her phone buzzed. He handed it back to her, she checked to see what had come in. It was another email. She brought it up and gasped.

Laszlo leaned closer. The words were the same: *Stop now, bitch.* But below it was a cartoon image of a cat that had been beheaded. "This is exactly what I mean." He gently took the phone from her hand and held it out so Geir could see.

Geir nodded. "Yeah, that's how the trouble starts."

Laszlo glanced at her. "Do you mind if I forward this to my email?"

She looked at him in surprise and then shrugged. "Go

for it. Although I don't know why you'd care."

"Because we might be able to track the email address."

"We?" she asked quietly.

He motioned toward Geir. "*We* might be able to track it."

"What good will it do?"

"It could trace down the person sending these. You've had two today?"

She nodded. "One this morning and one just now."

"Anything else?"

Bewildered, she shrugged and looked around. "No, not really. I haven't been into the office all day. Partly because I've been avoiding the office, staying away from all the accusing looks, because, of course, everybody knows what I did."

"What? That you stood up to being harassed? And at a level that's not acceptable anywhere?"

She nodded. "The trouble is, the guy has been around for a long time. He's well-loved. He fought to get everybody raises. He fought to get everybody parental leave. As far as they're all concerned, he's a good guy."

"*Aah*. So you're the bad guy. He's the good guy, and, for whatever reason, your nose is in a snit, and you're just trying to make his life miserable?" Geir asked.

She nodded. "Yeah, that's about it. It's stupid. But they love him, and now I've made his life miserable."

"Don't suppose any other women may have left because of him?"

"Quite possibly. Two women left over the last year, but I don't know why. They didn't really give an excuse. They just upped and handed in their notices. Their reasons could be anything."

"What are their names?"

"Angela Davis and Melinda Barry. I did give the cop their names too." She frowned as Geir wrote it down. "You're not going to contact them, are you?"

"Ask the police if they did a follow-up."

"They did get other jobs, and they said they were moving on, although they both said the same thing, so I don't know if that was just an excuse." She stood. "Don't take it personally, but you two are now making me very nervous."

"Good," Laszlo said, his voice low but hard. "If it keeps you alive, then I don't care how nervous it makes you. And feel free to run away. But, if you get into trouble, make sure you call us."

"And you're presuming, of course, the problem will come tonight. You do realize that, after you guys leave, that's when the trouble will come?"

"We'll be in New Mexico. Less than seven hundred miles away. Not exactly a superlong drive but not around the corner," he admitted. "Let's hope this guy will be content with sending you nasty emails."

She pocketed her phone, shot them both a look, turned to face Agnes coming around to the cash register where she paid her bill, and then, without another word to anyone, walked out to her vehicle.

SHE GOT INTO her small Subaru, backed out of the parking lot and headed onto the main street.

Laszlo watched her disappear. "Wish we knew where she lived."

"Yeah. You're getting the same bad feeling I am."

Laszlo hated to admit it, but he was. "The problem is, like she said, the trouble may not come tonight. It might not come for a day or two days or a week ..."

"Or never," Geir said. "Let's stay positive. For all we know, this will die down."

"And who would be the one to do something like this?"

"The guy who might be charged? Somebody he loves. Somebody who loves him? Or is he somebody who would hire someone?"

"Hard to say. A lot of people, if they like him, won't want to see his life slurred like this, but he needs to stop."

"Sexual harassment is never appropriate. If it's not Minx, he could go after many other women. And that should not be allowed. And although he didn't attack her or force her into anything, he made it fairly explicit how he felt about it. And don't forget she had her job transferred, so she's the one being punished, not him."

"Who are y'all talking about now?" Agnes asked. She stood beside them. She was amazingly silent for her bulk as she glared at them.

Laszlo looked up at her. "You have good hearing."

She nodded. "I do at that. And I always keep an ear to the ground for the people I care about." She motioned in the direction Minx had left. "And that girl has had enough trouble in her life."

"We're not trying to cause more trouble," Laszlo said. "She's just got a packet full of it. She doesn't realize how bad it could get."

Agnes dropped her meaty fists onto the table and leaned forward. "Explain," she barked.

Laszlo did, and, when he was done, she stared at him for a long moment and then gave a quick nod. "Then you best be keeping an eye on her, hadn't you?"

"We leave in the morning," Laszlo protested but without much heat because he couldn't ignore that Minx might be in trouble. Spunky though she was, it might not be enough. "We also have work we need to do."

"Well, what if you had some angle or something to tug on Mouse's background? Would that keep you around for another day or two?" she asked rudely. "And, at the same time, you can hunt down whoever it is doing this to Minx."

Geir stared at her. "And do you know more about Mouse's background than you're letting on?"

She slid him a look and said, "Maybe."

Laszlo believed her. "Deal. We can stay for another day or two if something's worth sticking around for."

She shook her head. "Nope, you got to agree to help Minx."

"It can't be open-ended," Laszlo pointed out. "We leave at some point."

"At some point?" she pounced. "That hotel is mine too. And you boys are there tonight. You can stay tomorrow night for free too."

Laszlo raised his eyebrows. "Quite the businesswoman, aren't you?"

But shrewd eyes studied him. "I already checked that you were registered there and your names. I had friends run your backgrounds once I heard you were looking for Mouse." Her voice deepened with each word spoken. "We don't let none of our friends get hurt. So, is that a deal or no deal?"

Laszlo and Geir looked at each other. Geir shrugged. "We can stay another day and another night. After that, by noon of the next day, we'll be on the road."

She nodded. "By then Minx will have it taken care of." And with that entirely mystic and confusing statement, she turned and walked away as she tossed over her shoulder, "Lunch is on us."

Realizing they'd been dismissed, and in a way taken advantage of, the two got up, called back, "Thanks. It was excellent." Then they both left the building. Outside, they stood for a long moment, neither saying anything. Laszlo pulled on his glove, thinking about what just happened.

Geir said finally, "Is this not one of the most bizarre situations we've ever ended up in?"

"Now that we apparently have some PI work to do for the next day and a half, we need to figure out what we'll do."

"Except she didn't give us any information on Mouse."

Just then Bart walked around from the back of the building and called out, "Laszlo."

Laszlo walked toward him. "You're the one with the information?"

Bart nodded. "Mouse's mother was my sister. Piece of shit that she was. And I had almost nothing to do with her. But her kid was okay."

"Your sister?" Laszlo couldn't believe anybody would let his nephew go through the kind of life Mouse had had without stepping in. Especially given the size of Bart.

He shook his head. "Make that stepsister. I never had nothing to do with her from the time she was ten until about thirty. I didn't even know Mouse was family until we got to talking one time. The kid was already a teen. He was getting big enough to handle himself then, but I went and had a talk with my stepsister, scared the bejesus out of her into leaving the kid alone. Had to do it a couple times. She'd be decent for a little while, and then she wouldn't be. By then Mouse was ready to leave."

"He came here a lot?"

Bart nodded. "He sat at the table in the back room often. Then so did Minx, especially if Mouse was working."

"You fed them and listened to them."

"As much as we could. Once in a while I'd call the cops to talk to the bitch. Only Mouse would tell the cops how everything was okay. When I asked him what the hell he was doing, he said he didn't want to get his mama in trouble. So, what are you supposed to do with that? He was almost grown. I didn't even know how bad things were until he broke down one day and told me. But even then when I called the cops, he wouldn't back up what he'd said. Some people are like that."

"So, what else can you tell us that'll help us get into his background more? Do you know anything about his father?"

"He is a mystery, but there was a stepfather for a few years. He took his own son and left. Mouse wasn't his supposedly. At least that was the garbled version I got from Mouse."

"Do you have a name?"

"Yarmouth," Bart said. "George Yarmouth."

"Any idea where he lives?"

He shook his head. "No. But if you're the PI types, you can roust that information out."

"Did the kids ever have anything to do with each other?"

"I don't think so. But who the hell knows? Mouse did have a boyfriend. He didn't want Minx to know too early on because he didn't want her to feel bad or ashamed or look at him any different. Agnes and me, we didn't care none. As long as he was happy, healthy, and enjoying safe sex, then he could have it any which way he found it."

Laszlo nodded. "It still couldn't have been easy on Mouse though."

"No. Some asshole, an older guy, took advantage of him."

"Which would have been rape if anybody had spoken up about it."

"Exactly. You got to think, in the neighborhood they were raised, rape happened at every street corner. There was no end and no stopping most of it. Mouse's mom, I hate to say it, but she was one of the worst. If Mouse had been a girl, she probably would have run her into prostitution as her pimp. And a hell of a lot earlier than Mouse's first experience. The whole family is bad news."

"So, she's your stepsister? Are there more siblings? Did Mouse have other uncles, cousins?"

"Stepsister. My father married her mother. Didn't last very long. I'm sure you can see why. The apple didn't fall far from the tree. And no siblings for either of us. Both mothers were addicts and living a never-ending cycle of abuse."

"It's a hard life for anybody."

"It is. But at some point the abuse cycle has to stop."

"Any idea who the boyfriend is?"

"Lance. But I don't know his last name."

"It was a long time ago, it's no wonder."

"I should though. His daddy was a rich man in town."

"Any idea what business he was in?"

Bart stared off in the distance. Suddenly the door banged behind him, and Agnes stepped out. Bart growled, "Who the hell was Lance's father?"

"Smithson," she said. "They owned the string of jewelry stores in town here."

Laszlo glanced over at Geir who was busy writing notes.

"Okay, we might be back asking more questions. This will give us a place to start." He stopped, reached into his pocket, pulled out a notepad, wrote down his phone number, also Geir's, and handed it over. "If you come up with anything else, let us know."

"Mouse was a good kid," Bart said.

Laszlo nodded. "We agree. He was one of us." He spoke quietly, almost in reverence. "That he died is something we're all suffering over. But he became a good man."

They both beamed as if they were proud of their own son. On that note, Laszlo and Geir headed to their vehicle.

Geir stopped and looked back, asking, "Was there only one boyfriend?"

Agnes and Bart looked at each other, and Bart shrugged, then added, "He stayed in touch with his first sexual encounter."

Laszlo froze. "With the man who abused him?"

"Mouse would never have said it was abuse. Seduction, yes. The man was a father figure to him."

"I don't suppose you know who that was, do you?"

Agnes nodded. "Hell yeah, I do. He's bad news. He's been in and out of jail constantly."

Laszlo waited.

She took a deep breath and said, "JoJo. JoJo Henderson." And she reeled off an address. "That's the last place I heard he was living. It's a halfway house for cons. He's more popularly known as Poppy."

"You think they might have still stayed in touch over the years?"

"In a very twisted way, Mouse was grateful to him. So I wouldn't be at all surprised."

On that note the two café owners turned around and

moved inside, the door closing behind them with a soft *clank*.

Laszlo stared at Geir. "Did you ever hear the like?"

Geir shook his head. "I'm beginning to wonder if we knew Mouse at all."

CHAPTER 7

A S MINX DROVE home, her mind was consumed with the warnings from Laszlo and Geir. She wasn't sure what to think of the two men. They'd seemed sincere—dedicated and hard-working military types. But there was more to it than that. A lot of men would never have come looking for Mouse two years after his death. She understood they hadn't been capable of coming to see about him before. But it was still an odd thing.

She didn't want to think about the explosion not being an accident. But Mouse had lived a hard life. And she probably didn't want to know how hard. She was surprised Agnes had talked to them, though she hadn't said much. It was a sign Agnes trusted them, which Minx had to admit, she didn't have any reason not to. But they were still strangers. And stranger-danger was something she'd learned as a toddler. But the men made good suggestions, and it had definitely scared the crap out of her to not take any of this too lightly. As she had that thought, she pulled into the corner store to pick up a few things.

On her way back out she noticed a beat-up old Ford truck off to the side. She was pretty damn sure she'd seen that vehicle at Agnes's restaurant. She got in her car and drove back out. In the main stream of traffic, she looked behind her several times, but there was no sign of it. She smiled and settled back. Laszlo had instilled just enough fear in her.

Just as she was about to make the next turn, taking the upcoming exit off the freeway into her neighborhood, she saw the pickup behind her. She frowned, but it was already too late to change her course. She took the turnoff and watched as the truck came in behind her. Shit.

Only one person was in the cab. Tall, very tall, she could barely see his head through the darkened windshield. So not Laszlo and/or Geir. Both were big men, but she could already see it wasn't them.

Refusing to go to her apartment, she drove around the block several times, then started to weave, looking to shake the tail. But, instead of being shaken off, he stayed right on her. Scared, she wasn't sure what the hell to do. She pulled out her phone, ready to call 9-1-1. She took a left and then another left and then realized she was just circling the block.

She headed back out on the freeway and managed to catch a yellow light, slipping in just under the red. But, as she thought she'd made it without any chance of him following, he'd run the red light among all the roaring horns. And once again, he was right on her ass.

Her fingers shaking, she looked at her phone, trying to drive and dial Laszlo's number.

"Hello?"

"Somebody's tailing me," she said, half shrieking. "I've tried several times to shake him off, but he won't disappear. And he's not making any attempt to hide."

"Where are you?"

"On the freeway heading toward Northrop."

"I'm putting that into the GPS, as this isn't my town. Are you almost at home?"

"I was. I drove around the block several times, so he wouldn't see exactly where I live, but he followed me every time. So I headed back into the heavy traffic. I tried to get in under a yellow light, thinking he wouldn't follow, but he ran the red light."

"Do you see a coffee shop, a public place, a police station, anything up ahead?"

Taking the closest exit off the freeway, she hunted through the dim lights. It was dusky right now. Streetlights had come on, but she hated this time for trying to see anything. "A coffee shop might be up ahead, if it's still there. I'm going by memory here."

"Drive toward it and let us know."

She peered through the windshield to see if it was there. "It's still here," she cried out.

"Okay, what's the street?"

"Stanton. I'm pulling in."

"Park between two vehicles if you can, so he can't park beside you."

"I'm parking right in front of the street-facing window. At least if anybody sees him trying anything, they'll see me screaming."

"I don't want you going in. I want you to remain in your car," he snapped.

"How far away are you?"

"Possibly ten minutes. But Geir is driving, so it could be half that."

"Don't hang up on me," she pleaded.

"I won't," he said, his manner calm, reassuring. "Where's the truck now?"

"It just came off the highway behind me. He's circling the coffee shop's parking lot, looking for a place to pull in."

"Keep an eye on it without getting out of the vehicle. Make sure your doors are locked, and, if you're feeling very uncomfortable, you can slump down and hide on the seat."

"I think that would be worse. I'd be waiting to see if his face appeared in my windshield."

"At least we'd find out what he looked like."

"I know. I know. Oh, he's coming around again," she cried out. She half slid down on the seat as he drove behind her. "He's gone to the other side of the parking lot. He just passed behind me."

"Any idea if he was looking your way?"

"No, he didn't appear to be. He just seems to be looking for a parking spot." She took a deep breath. "Am I making too much out of this?"

"No way to know," he said in a very soothing and calm voice. "And this is not the time to question yourself."

"He's parked at the far end."

"Okay. Just sit there and watch him."

"He's not getting out."

"Can you read the license plate?"

"No, not at all."

"We're taking the turnoff coming into the coffee shop area from a different angle. I want you to direct me to where he is parked so I can park somewhere close by, and we can grab the license plate."

It took her a minute to realize what he was asking, then she said, "There's an entrance and exit to the parking lot from the main road and the side street." She quickly gave them directions. "What are you driving?"

"My truck. It's a Dodge Ram, half-ton, silver."

"Okay, I remember it."

"We're driving into the parking lot now," he said.

"So pick any of the spots on the right." She spotted the truck as it came in. "He's right behind you."

"Got him. You stay where you are. I'll come and get you."

She hung up her phone, her heart pounding. She wrung her hands together as she stared through the windshield. What if the asshole bolted?

She watched as the Dodge pickup parked. And, sure enough, Laszlo and Geir hopped out. They walked around the back of the building.

When they were out of sight from the truck's view, she hopped out and moved around to the far edge of the coffee shop. She ran toward them and reached out. Laszlo gripped her hands and tugged her in for a quick hug. She clung to him for a long moment, overwhelmingly relieved to have him here. He just held her. Then he whispered, "The truck is still parked there. We've got the license plate."

"But he might take off now," she cried out, stepping back to look at him, then at Geir.

"Nobody was in it," Geir said. "Did you see anybody get out?"

She shook her head. "No. But I don't know. He might have opened the door, and I wouldn't have been able to see."

"It would have been easy enough for him to have crouched down and used the other vehicles to hide behind. Another vehicle coming in could have hidden his passage across, and he could have come around the coffee shop to go inside."

He motioned to the coffee shop and said, "Let's get a cup of coffee, and we'll talk." But he kept his arm tight around her shoulders. It was both comforting and irritating. But the comfort part won out.

She looked at him. "I can walk on my own, you know?"

He nodded. "But it's much better if this guy doesn't think you're alone."

Instantly she realized he was trying to offer her protection. She sighed. "I can't tell if I'm supposed to be spitting mad because of what he did or look at myself as a screaming, lily-white, hand-wringing, useless female and get angry at myself for being reduced to this."

"And what will you do about it?" Geir asked with interest. "Have you had much experience with being followed?"

"Too much," she said in a dark tone. "But not when driving."

Both men looked at her.

She shrugged. "I wasn't kidding when I said I had to hide from predators. You learn those lessons very young."

"Sounds like a lovely childhood."

"It wasn't. But I left. It's one of the reasons I was so happy Mouse got out. Don't misunderstand. ... Initially I felt betrayed and abandoned, but, over time, I was glad he made it out of here."

"I'm surprised you stayed as long as you did."

"It wasn't even a case of staying. I knew, if I left school and got a job, I'd never go back to school. That's why I contacted my uncle. As soon as I could get the hell out. And, by then, you have to realize my mother was mostly drugged out anyway."

"Where would she get the money for drugs?"

Minx shot him a sideways look. "How do most female drug addicts get money for drugs?" She paused. "Hell, the same way male drug addicts do, I suppose."

Neither man said anything. They nodded quietly.

"I tried hard to help her. But, at some point, you realize

there's nothing you can do."

They nodded again. She liked that about the men. They got it. First time around. No explanation needed. And no need to make small talk.

Once inside the restaurant, she took a quick survey of the customers but didn't see any suspicious-looking guy anywhere. "If we sit over there, we can see both sides of the restaurant."

Laszlo nodded. "Good thinking."

They sat down. She didn't want any more coffee.

Laszlo said, "I'm going to the front and getting a coffee. Do you want one?"

She didn't but she nodded anyway. "Yes, please."

Geir sat across from her. He had a notepad out and was jotting down more things.

"Considering we haven't talked much, you've taken a lot of notes."

"Agnes offered us some more information after you left."

She felt her jaw drop. "Agnes did?"

He nodded. "I gather from your expression that she doesn't share much?"

"Agnes doesn't trust anybody. And she shares even less."

"She wanted something in return for the information though."

"Yeah, that would be Agnes. Although what she would want, I have no idea."

He shrugged. "It wasn't anything. We were happy to help."

Just then Laszlo returned. He placed two cups of coffee on the table. "I'll be right back."

She looked at him and saw that, of course, he hadn't been able to carry three cups.

"I should have gone with him," she murmured, watching as he returned to the counter.

"He's a big boy," Geir said, still writing. "He can handle the pain of a second trip."

That surprised a laugh out of her. "Hardly sympathetic," she said.

He chuckled. "I've known him for well over a decade. We know exactly what we can do."

"And that's probably a good thing."

"It is. That goes along with having a support system. It's like, when you do call for help, people know exactly what help you need. We don't call without reason, and, when we do, everybody jumps to help."

She sighed happily. "Sounds lovely," she admitted.

"It is, but it didn't get there overnight."

"Do you see anybody here it could be?" she said out of the blue.

"Two possible," he said, without looking up. "One on the other side of the restaurant. Both wearing short-sleeve cotton plaid shirts, both males sitting alone at tables. Big, big, big as in 280 pounds, six foot, looks rough, maybe like a trucker. The other one is big at six, maybe six one, but he's got a full head of hair, making him look bigger. Plus he's rolled up the short sleeves on his shirt even shorter to accentuate his biceps."

She stared at Geir. "How do you know all that?"

"I just looked."

She shot him a resentful glance. "Apparently your version of looking is very different than mine."

He chuckled at that. "Apparently."

LASZLO WALKED BACK over, having taken a different route through the restaurant this time with the idea of looking at the glass case of goodies in the front. He certainly wasn't hungry after Agnes's big burger and fries, but it let him walk a different path back to the table.

"It's the guy on the left," he said to Geir.

Geir nodded. "That's what I was thinking."

"What are you talking about?"

"The guy who's got more hair, making him look taller, whose shirt collar is jacked up, making him look bigger. Whether he does that to intimidate others or he likes to think he's a big man, I don't know."

"Or it happens to be the only clean shirt he could get his hands on before he walked out the door," she snapped. She shook her head. "Do you guys always analyze everything?"

"Sure," Laszlo said. "Keeps us in practice."

"Practice for what?"

Neither man said a word.

She raised both hands in mock surrender. "Okay, so if that's him, what do we do?"

"We wait and we watch."

"And then what? I can't just sit here the whole time. I need some sleep tonight. Tomorrow is another workday."

"And does that mean you'll go in dressed-down again?"

"Maybe," she admitted. "But I'll be in a different area tomorrow. I wanted to check out a couple files I have and the houses they're living in." After that the topic returned to Agnes. "What did she tell you about Mouse?" Minx asked. "I'm really shocked that she talked to you."

"She gave us the name of the boyfriend and the name of the man who first sexually abused Mouse. We have to consider that Mouse stayed in contact with him all this time."

She gasped and settled back against her seat. "He what?"

"Bart also confirmed Mouse had a stepfather. That man came into the relationship with a child of his own but left when Mouse was still a child. According to Bart and Agnes, Mouse wasn't that father's child."

"Right. As I said before though, I don't know the details." She raised a brow. "And what are you doing in exchange for that information?"

Laszlo stared at her. When she motioned toward Geir, he understood. "Agnes wants us to make sure you're okay for the next day or two."

"What?" she stared at them in shock. "Did you tell her?"

"Just about the phone messages. That's all we knew. She already knew about the sexual harassment case."

Minx sank back into her seat yet again. "That's the thing about Agnes. You can't tell her anything she doesn't already know."

"She really cares about you and wants to make sure you stay safe."

Minx stared moodily out the window. "I think I need to move." Then she snorted angrily. "Why the hell should I? It's his damn fault. I'd have stayed happy in my job but for him."

"You don't have to move," Laszlo said. "If you love your job, your home, have friends and family to stay close to, then don't."

"Other than Agnes and Bart, no friends or family I'd stay for," she said, her voice frustrated, angry. "I don't know how I feel, but I don't want to continue working for the city. Not sure that I do want to stay. I'm just confused."

"Yet you keep saying something along those lines. Pick a

place, hand in your notice and then move."

She slid forward again toward him. "What about that job part? Shouldn't I be looking for a job first? Wait until I get hired and then move?"

"You could do it that way. Or you could pick a place to move, take a month to settle in, figure out where you want to work and then apply."

"That's how I ended up here. I left my uncle's place in Maine and moved to my friend's place here, and that didn't work out so well."

"What did you do back in Maine?"

"I was a student doing typical age-related jobs. Waitressing, worked in a garden shop for a while." She shrugged. "I needed money."

"And why did you and your friend fall out?"

She winced. "Because my friend from way back hadn't given up one of her more unpleasant hobbies."

The men stopped and stared.

She shrugged. "When younger she used sex to get the extras in life. Now she uses sex to get everything in life."

"She's a prostitute?"

"A high-end call girl is what she would call it."

"I don't suppose she wanted you to go into the business by any chance, did she?"

"Oh, yeah. She sure did. Didn't take it kindly when I made it very clear after several months of beating around the bush, not really understanding what she was doing with her life. Not until she came flat-out and told me how unimpressed she was that I'd been living there free of charge for three months while I looked for a job. The thing is, I'd been staying there rent free, but I had been paying for all the groceries, doing all the cleaning, running all the errands, everything while she was off in all these mysterious meetings."

"How long did it take you to figure it out?"

"Way too long," she said shortly. "She had lots of groups she belonged to, a major social life she was a part of. And a boyfriend. So I was happy to just play along and not get too involved. I was excited about being around her again, having a connection to my past. But finally I got suspicious. At that point, I sent out lots of job applications. I didn't want to go back to my uncle's, as if I'd failed. I ended up getting a job as a counselor at a private school, but she told me the job would never pay what she made, and I should jump ship and join her. The next day I had my own apartment. By the weekend I was in it and long gone from her world." She chuckled. "I saw too much of that shit growing up. No way was I going there. Besides, I moved into my current job soon afterward."

"Did you tell the cops about her?"

She shook her head. "No, I didn't. Maybe I should have, though."

"Sometimes it's best not to interfere."

CHAPTER 8

MINX EXITED HER car and walked over to the small basement apartment she had rented. She pulled out her keys and slipped them inside the doorknob. She did not look behind her. She knew both men were even now watching her arrival. They would follow her inside the apartment within seconds, so, even if somebody waited for her, chances were good she wouldn't be in danger. As soon as they told her their plan, she just about had a heart attack. But she'd immediately seen the sense of it and had agreed.

Inside she turned on the lights, and, unable to stop herself, she quickly did a walk-through of her apartment, checking the closets and under the bed. But found no sign of anyone. Relieved, she placed her keys and purse atop the kitchen table and waited until the men joined her. She didn't need more coffee, but a cup of tea might help chase away the irritation and fatigue she felt. She'd call it stress, but it seemed like her life had been filled with nothing but stress recently, ever since her asshole of a boss had decided he wanted a whole lot more from her than she wanted to give.

With the teakettle boiling, she took off her shoes and dropped onto the couch. There was still no sign of the men. She had no idea what they could find to do out there, but they appeared to be thorough. That they weren't on her heels made her worry they'd found something.

When a knock came on the door a few moments later, she got up and answered, "Who's there?"

"It's me," Laszlo said. "Let us in."

She opened the door to them.

He studied her door. "There's no peephole?"

She shrugged. "Nope, there isn't. But then it's lacking a whole lot more than that too." She opened the door wide enough for them to come in. It seemed strange to have these larger-than-life men in her small space. It was almost as odd as the space itself. It was not home and not a hotel but somewhere in between.

They did a quick walk-through, like she had but, in some ways, more thorough. Of course this was their first time seeing the place. They moved like predators on the prowl. Smooth, loose-limbed and powerful. She could watch Laszlo for hours; he was so beautiful in his movements. What did that say about her?

"You rented it furnished?"

She nodded slowly, pulling herself together, crossing her arms and leaning against the living room wall that separated the living room from the kitchen area. "Why?"

"You didn't have any of your own furniture?"

"I have an apartment on the other side of the city. But it's way longer of a commute than I wanted with this newest job. So I rented this basement suite on a short-term basis. I was hoping to make this an extremely short transfer. But every time I ask when it's over, I keep getting the same song and dance."

"And were you planning on going back to your old position?"

"When I started this process, I thought that might be doable, but apparently I'm naive because everybody else hated me for what I accused Andrew of."

"Andrew who?"

"Andrew Conley. He's my old boss with the wandering fingers, vicious gaze and expectations way beyond reality."

The men nodded and wrote down his name. "Do you have a copy of the report you signed?"

"Remember I go in tomorrow and sign it?"

"That's kind of odd. Normally you would sign a statement right off the bat."

"That's probably my fault. They offered me a chance to consider what I was doing and to think about if I was really serious about going through with it."

"Isn't this a criminal offense?" Laszlo frowned. "Surely there's no choice at this point."

"Well, I would have thought so," she said. "But I guess they wanted me to be sure I was prepared to go through with this. Maybe they have had a rash of false sexual harassment accusations lately."

Laszlo said, "They often drop the charges if the defendant isn't willing to testify."

She nodded. "Exactly."

"You decided you were?"

She shrugged. "Thinking about not testifying wasn't making me sleep at night. Because I kept thinking of all the other women he would do this to. Women who needed the job and felt they had to comply in order to keep it. An amazing number of single mothers' security is threatened in that very manner. And it's not right."

"True enough. What time is your appointment?"

"At ten a.m." She got up as the teakettle whistled, walked over and made herself a cup of tea. Did they want something? She turned to look at the men. "You don't look like tea-drinkers, but can I make you a cup?"

Both men shook their heads.

She smiled. "I'm sorry. I don't have any alcohol in the house."

"It's not a problem."

Just then one of the men's phones went off. She watched as Laszlo pulled his phone from his pocket and smiled.

"We have a rundown on the license plate. The vehicle was stolen four days ago." Laszlo put his phone back in his pocket.

She picked up her tea, walked to the living room, sat down carefully and held her drink close, needing the warmth, the comfort of just the hot tea against her chest. "Stolen?"

"Yes, likely stolen for the purpose of following you. Who were you talking to at the police station?"

"Officer Charter," she answered. "But I doubt this would have anything to do with him."

He nodded. "I know somebody who might be able to help us."

"Levi?" Geir asked.

Laszlo nodded. "I know they work closely with the Houston law enforcement officers."

"Maybe one of them can recommend somebody here?"

He had his phone out again and hit a couple buttons on it while she watched. When somebody answered on the other end, he said, "Levi, it's Laszlo."

She half listened in on the conversation while they explained where they were. "I'm sure you know why we're here, but we met an old neighborhood friend of Mouse's, only she's being tailed. She filed a sexual harassment report on her boss a few days ago. And she's going in tomorrow to sign the paperwork to go through with the allegations. We just tracked the license plate number on the truck tailing her to a vehicle stolen four days ago." He listened for a few moments. "That's what we were thinking,"

She tuned out the conversation, put her teacup on the coffee table and curled up in the corner of the couch. Geir took one look, grabbed a folded blanket off the side and held it out for her. She smiled, nodded and wrapped it around her shoulders. She just wanted this all to go away. As a matter of fact, she wanted everything to go away. It seemed like, since she had returned to Texas, her life had not been how she'd hoped.

So why had she stayed? Because she had no place to go? Well, she did. She could return to Maine, but that didn't feel right either. She was supposed to make her own way now. And that seemed to be almost impossible when she kept running up against shitty scenarios.

Finally Laszlo got off the phone and turned toward her, his gaze narrow. "He'll make a couple calls, see if he can get somebody to deal with us. I also gave him the license plate number and told him where the vehicle was. It's not likely to still be there, but the fact that he parked it, and we never saw him or the truck leaving, it's possible it was ditched."

"You don't think it was the second man from the restaurant?"

"He drove off in a small car just as we were leaving," Geir said. "It's possible he had nothing to do with this. It's also possible he was a diversion at the restaurant or came in another vehicle so you wouldn't notice."

She shivered. "I'm not that important. A sexual harassment lawsuit wouldn't be *that* devastating to anyone," she snapped. "Why would somebody go to all the trouble?"

"There's no way to tell, but it would likely cost him his job, his reputation, perhaps his wife … family," Laszlo said.

"But he's a nobody. He's not married, not that I know of. And what reputation? He works for the city in some low-level midmanagement position. Although I did hear he was active in his church, go figure."

"But you've started a process, and now we carry on and see how it'll go."

"I hear you, but this isn't how I want to live my life."

The men chuckled. "That's the thing about life. It lives you, not you living it."

That startled a laugh out of her. "So now what? You guys take off for the night, and I stay here, and, when I get up in the morning, I go to the cops and hopefully nobody's following me then?"

"I'll stay here," Laszlo said. "Geir can return to our hotel room. I'll make sure you're okay for the night, and I'll go with you to the cops in the morning. If somebody's trying to stop you from going forward with this complaint, then you'll need protection until you get there. Though that doesn't mean you won't need protection afterward as well."

Geir shrugged. "Police corruption can be pretty ugly. It's one of the reasons we contacted Levi. He knows decent people, at least in Houston. He might know somebody in Dallas. What we need is a cop we can trust. Did you speak to anybody else about the problem?"

She shook her head. "No, just the cop I'm supposed to meet tomorrow."

"Then I'm definitely going with you because I want to get the measure of this man," Laszlo said. "Any more thoughts on moving?"

"I've done nothing but think about it," she said. "But it

doesn't change the fact I have no clue where to move to. And I still need a job."

"Is your other apartment rented out?"

She nodded. "I sublet it to a friend who's in town for a few weeks. Just long enough for me to sort myself out, I hope."

It was obvious the men understood.

A few minutes later, Geir held out his hand, and Laszlo tossed him the keys. "Where's the station?" Geir asked.

She shrugged. "The one on Second Avenue."

He nodded. "I'll see you both there, ten in the morning." He glanced at Laszlo. "We've got one more night, but let me know if you want me to bring anything for you here in the morning."

Laszlo got to his feet. "Sounds good." He nodded his head to Minx. "I'll walk him out. I'll be back in a minute. Lock the door and stay inside until I come back."

Tired, unnerved at the thought he was staying with her—and at the thought he didn't even ask, it was just a recognized thing that had to happen—she got up and threw the bolt behind them. She didn't know how long they would be, but she figured it was close enough to bedtime that she could get ready and disappear pretty fast once he was back inside. She didn't want him thinking anything was going on between them. Not that he'd even made a move in that direction. But, like she'd said earlier, she hadn't gotten to this age without understanding how quickly things could change …

OUTSIDE LASZLO SAID, "Stay in touch. I have no idea how

this night will go."

"I'll drive past the coffee shop and see if the truck is still there. If it is, I'll call the cops again, make sure they come and pick it up. Whoever owns that vehicle could probably use it. And, of course, we didn't get the license plate of the red car, the one the man drove off in."

Laszlo shook his head. "Typical, right? We're focused on one, and they get up and leave in a different one."

"And it could be that he had nothing to do with it."

Laszlo nodded. "But somebody drove the truck."

"I'm pretty sure he just deserted it and walked away. It was enough that she knew he'd followed her. He wouldn't stick around to be identified."

"Scare tactics?"

Geir nodded. "Sounds like it to me."

"That's not helpful. If those antics don't stop her from going to the police again tomorrow, he'll just change his tack and come back."

"I know." Geir walked over to the truck, hopped in and said out the open window, "Have a good night." He flashed Laszlo a big grin and drove away.

Laszlo walked back to the apartment, his gaze studying the floor above. He couldn't see anything inside as it was dark. She'd said nobody was staying there at the moment, but it would be a perfect cover for anybody wanting to torment her, or worse, attack her. He'd already taken a walk around the block to get an idea of where she lived. It was low- to middle-class suburbia. Lots of rental units but then everybody had to have a way to pay the mortgage.

Back at her door he knocked on the wood and waited until she opened it. It took her a minute. He wondered if he needed to rap again when she pulled it open. She was dressed in pajamas, wearing a bathrobe. He smiled broadly. She stepped aside and let him in.

He walked back in, taking his shoes off at the door. "Tired?"

"Very. There's nothing like the aftermath of fear and shock to take the stuffing out of me."

"It's a normal reaction for everyone," he said.

She shrugged. "The trouble is, I'm not everyone. For a long time, I lived in that state. But I've been out of it too long. I don't want to go back into it either."

He nodded. "It sounds like you had some pretty close calls."

"A couple in particular, and it was always Mouse who saved me. That's why it was so hard when he left. I was just hitting puberty, and I knew I was in more danger than ever. A lot of my mother's boyfriends didn't like children. And that was something to be grateful for. But a lot of them wouldn't have known the difference between a fourteen-year-old and an eighteen-year-old, and most of them wouldn't have cared."

He winced.

She nodded. "Some of us had shitty beginnings."

"But you escaped it. You got an education and changed your life," he reminded her. He looked at the teakettle. "Can I change my mind on that cup of tea?"

She nodded. "Absolutely. Help yourself."

He walked into the kitchen, shook the electric teakettle to find water was still inside and pushed the button to start heating it up again. "Where would I find tea and a cup?"

He followed her directions and soon had a hot cup of tea. He moved back to the living room, sitting down. He assessed the length of the couch and realized it would probably be more comfortable if he crashed on the floor.

"I don't have much to offer in the way of bedding," she said. "When I said this place came complete, I meant it. I brought a suitcase of my belongings, and that's it."

He shrugged. "I've had worse."

"Let me see if I have an extra blanket." She headed into her bedroom and came back out with a blanket that had been on her bed. "It's not like it's cold. I don't need the comforter and the blanket, so you can have this for the night."

"Good enough." He stretched out on the couch, while she sat in the armchair. "I don't know if you wanted to go straight to bed. If so, go ahead, get some sleep. Just be aware, I'll get up every couple hours and take a walk around, make sure everything's okay."

"Outside?"

He shook his head. "Inside."

She nodded, but it was obvious she wanted to leave. He motioned to her bedroom. "Go. I don't need you here to entertain me. I've got my laptop. I'll get some work done."

She stopped on her way to the bedroom and looked back at him.

He already had his laptop open and his feet up on the coffee table. He took off his glove and quickly started flicking through emails. "Have a good night."

She hesitated another long moment, then said, "Good night."

He waited until she went into her room and closed the door. Then he relaxed. She was wary, very wary. And that was okay. He had no designs on her. He just wanted to keep her safe. After that, ... well, ... who knew? Still, he wasn't staying in town, so it wasn't likely to go anywhere. Besides, two years after his accident, he wasn't looking to jump into a serious relationship. Not yet.

He felt rusty. Unsure. Even more considering his less-than-stellar physical condition. But he was more than happy to look at her and after her.

That Mouse had spent a lot of time and effort looking after her said a lot about who Mouse was. That whole terrified-of-water thing was odd. Some of the BUD/S training they went through was extreme. He didn't under-stand how bad Mouse's fear of water was, but Laszlo knew, in many cases, it was not something people could get over quickly. He wondered if it would be possible to talk to the BUD/S instructors about Mouse's performance. Then what could he ask—Mouse had passed and water trials were some of the most grueling in the training. So he had to have done well.

He did a bit of research on getting over the fear, but nothing changed his attitude on the process. It was really just a matter of *face your fears and carry on.* But, of course, they wanted you to do it in a safe environment. But, if you couldn't even think of getting into a swimming pool or walking past a creek, then how did one get past that?

Just then he got an email from Geir.

Back at the hotel, checking in with everyone. So far nothing new popping up. Still researching Mouse's family. And you?

He responded in kind.

Yes, working on that now. Still flummoxed over the fear-of-water thing.

I know. Any chance we have two Mouses?

I highly doubt it with a name like that.

Brother?

Possible, then what happened to the real Mouse?

And why would you take over such a horrible life?

It doesn't make a whole lot of sense. We need to track down the family and talk to them.

I'm working on it, but there doesn't appear to be a whole lot of information available.

Or on Mouse's childhood. I can't find any hospital records, no dental records, nothing about school.

Right? It's almost as if he were a ghost. But I know, in many areas like this, people don't have medical insurance. And can walk in, get treatment, pay cash, then walk out without leaving a trace.

Laszlo went back to his research at that point, trying to find what he could on Lance. And that meant the jewelry store family. Laszlo quickly started digging into that family history. The aged patriarch was old German and apparently hadn't had much tolerance for his grandson's sexual preferences. He had tried to get him to join the family business until he realized the life he was leading, and then he'd been dumped. Lance's own father was part of the business, and, of course, it had been assumed his eldest son would go into it too. Lance had a younger brother, however, and he had stepped into the role instead. So Lance was allowed to lead his own life as long as it didn't impact the family's life.

There were lots of articles on him getting into trouble, but they were small incidences, never came with charges. Laszlo sent an email to Levi, asking if there was a way to check for a criminal record, explaining who Lance was in relation to Mouse. As it was still early, Levi came back fairly quickly with a copy of Lance's criminal record. Shoplifting, drugs, and … Wow, look at that. … Prostitution. How did somebody with a relative like his grandfather and father end up with prostitution charges?

But then Laszlo read farther and realized the charges

were dropped. He'd been caught up in a sting in a gay bar where they'd been looking for a pimp using young boys, a twist on the old story. The family had managed to get the charges dropped, paid all the fines in every case except apparently a drunk-driving case. But it carried jail time of only thirty days. The family hadn't been able to buy his way out of that one. And apparently drunk driving was more honorable than being caught in a drug or a prostitution sting.

But then many old families would have a problem with Lance's lifestyle. Laszlo wasn't shocked by any of it. So many of those with alternate lifestyles suffered persecution from those who didn't understand. Fear was a major factor. It was too bad because the Mouse who Laszlo knew had been a hell of a man. Mouse didn't deserve to be treated as anything less than an equal.

Laszlo kept clicking away on the keys as the bedroom door opened again. Minx walked out, looking frustrated and tired.

"Can't sleep?" he asked gently. She looked like a disgruntled kitten. Albeit one with claws.

She shook her head, walked over to the teakettle and plugged it in again. "I'm hoping a hot lemon will help."

"Anything in particular keeping you awake?"

She snorted. "There's plenty to choose from. I'm just seriously surprised anybody even gives a damn about me."

He stopped his research and took a look at her. "That brings up a good point then. Does your old boss care about his position? Is he so far away from retirement that he couldn't take a retirement package to have all this swept under the carpet, or do you think something else is going on?"

She shot him a troubling look, turned to get the lemon juice out of the fridge. She came back with the teacup in her hand and sat on the nearby chair, placing the hot lemon carefully on the side table. "I don't know. He was extremely blunt with me, as if he thought he had the right. As if this was his norm. That he wouldn't get into trouble regardless of what I said. Maybe if he'd kept on, he thought I'd buckle."

"Any chance he's gone beyond sexual harassment?"

"What do you mean?"

"Any chance he's raped somebody? Any chance he raped somebody under the legal age of consent?"

"How would I know? But he is slimy enough. And he's certainly aggressive enough." She frowned. "I just don't know why he would."

"Why he would what?"

"Put his career in jeopardy like that. But more than that, he's very active in his community and his church. I think he thought he was someone going places."

"Maybe it's that code-of-silence thing," he said. "A lot of women are too scared to fight back. They either quit or comply, leaving them likely to feel ashamed and angry. It's possible you're one of the few who hit back. What gets me is why he would have thought you wouldn't have. Since I first met you, you've been ..." He struggled to find the right word, knowing the wrong one would set her off. "Not abrasive but not exactly ... It's obvious you're no pushover. That's what puzzles me is that he must have thought otherwise."

CHAPTER 9

SHE STARED AT him. "That's true. But, when I first met you, I wasn't exactly my normal self. I was angry and hating the neighborhood where I'd grown up," she admitted. "I'm not always like that."

"But are you subservient? Are you the kind of person who lets people walk all over you?" He shook his head. "I can't fathom you would be so different in a work environment."

"No, I'm not. But I'm careful. I'm cautious. I didn't survive my childhood by being abrasive, and I didn't survive my childhood by being stupid. I keep my nose down, and I do my work."

"So maybe you were an unknown to him?" He appeared to think about that, then nodded. "That would make sense. He probably had already tested every other female in the office he could get his hands on, and you were something new. How long did you work there?"

"Under him, not long. Maybe four months. But I was in the building for quite a while."

"Did you know him before you took that position?"

She shook her head. "No, I didn't. I would go to work, do my job and leave. One of the things my upbringing taught me was to keep my nose clean. But that also meant not sticking it into other people's business. A lot of people are in that building, a couple hundred at least. And, over the years, I'd seen him, but I didn't know who he was, what his position was. He had moved up the ranks, so his position changed all the time." She shrugged. "Let's be clear though. He's big. His size could be intimidating. He's burly, but he's not pretty. He doesn't dress terribly well. He's much more of a trucker dressed up for an office job."

"Interesting analogy," he said. "I'm typing in his name to see if I can get an image of him."

"You should be able to." She got up, walked to the couch and sat down beside him.

He brought up the images that came with the name.

She reached over and tapped one photo. "That's him."

He clicked on the image and brought it up larger. "Isn't that interesting?"

"What?"

He shook his head. "He's got a hard edge to him. And arrogance. Almost as if he doesn't care or thinks he's too smart or thinks nobody will buck him. But there's also a sleazy salesman look to him. Sleeker than I expected."

"I just see the ugliness. He is arrogant," she said. "He doesn't think anybody has the guts to go against him."

"And yet you said he's well-loved?"

"He's done a lot for the employees."

"And is that also because management hasn't bucked him?"

She laughed. "Maybe. But nobody working under him in the offices really cares. If you think about it, as long as he's on their side, no employee will go against him."

Laszlo nodded. "The thing about guys like this—intimidating women in an office environment—it's all about power, and the guys don't expect to get caught. In his head, he's not doing anything a million other guys aren't doing. I understand that he's probably getting a thrill out of it. He's getting whatever bits and pieces of sex he needs to make him feel like a big man, to make him feel like he can have whatever he wants without anybody crossing him, but that seems kind of small change in the overall power-mad-hungry point of view. I just wonder if he's involved in something else. Those who are corrupt with power quite often would have other avenues that help them feel powerful too."

"I'm not sure I'm following you."

He looked at her. "You said you didn't think he was married, but is he divorced with an ex? Does he have kids? Does he have other people he intimidates? Is anyone scared of him?"

"I don't know if anyone is truly afraid of him. I know in the office there was a lot of adulation. It made me sick. I think I heard something about him being engaged," she murmured, frowning. "I don't know if he's ever been married. I have no clue if he has kids. I can't say I'd be surprised if he wasn't divorced. I doubt he would know the meaning of the wedding vows because he's a lecher. And, if he was married, then he probably abused her. Bullies are like that."

He nodded. "Exactly. She probably stayed home, raised their kids and everybody toed the line because, if they didn't, there would be a punishment. And now that I've seen his face, I can certainly understand he probably has hired whoever it was who tailed you today. Now whether that person would do anything other than keep track of your movements, I don't know. But I can see this Andrew guy doing whatever it takes to get you out of the picture."

She sank back in the couch and stared at him. "As in you

think he might kill me?"

"Not likely. That type of action means desperation. I can't say that he would or has before, but, if he's going after you now, and you're an unknown he can't figure out, and he might have misjudged you initially, he'll have to put a stop to it, won't he?"

"Sure, intimidation is usually effective," she said drily. "I mean, I've already lost my job and transferred into a lower position. But he's not seeing who I am on the inside. The one raised in a house beside Mouse."

He nodded. "And what happens next? You could get laid off? You could be fired? And it could just spiral downward from there."

"Meaning, if I don't stop harassing him now, then he could take stronger measures to get rid of me." She slowly let the breath out of her lungs. "Great. So my attempts to do right will just end up with me getting deeper into trouble."

"Don't suppose you have any proof, do you?"

She nodded. "I do actually." She got up and walked to the kitchen counter. There was a cookie tin on the side. She opened it and pulled out a small recorder. "After the first couple times, I realized how bad he was getting. I thought I should do something about it."

She sat down and played the tape. It was short, only two minutes. As Andrew's crude voice filled the air, she was more concerned about watching Laszlo's face to see his reaction than hearing the threats once more. They made her mad all over again.

"Wow, he's pretty clear what he wants you to do with him."

"Yeah, nice, huh? As if blow jobs go along with sorting the morning mail."

He chuckled. "If that was the case, most men would sign up for sorting the morning mail."

That startled a laugh out of her. "Now that may be. But it sure as hell isn't in my job description. I know I never signed up for that."

"Did you show this to the cops?"

She shook her head. "No. I can't say I got a warm and fuzzy feeling from the cops at all."

"No, it sounds like they were hoping you'd walk away from this and not proceed any further."

She nodded. "And that's not what I needed. I was really hoping somebody would be outraged and would want to go after this guy. Instead, I feel like I got a cop who didn't want to buck the system."

"Or who knew Andrew and knew maybe other charges were pending against him or other people were pissed off about him." Laszlo shrugged. "Or you could have just had a young cop who didn't know how to handle this."

"Well, you can bet he didn't ask anybody for advice," she said drily. She glanced over at the laptop. "What about Lance? Did you find out any more about his family?"

"Yeah. He did thirty days for drunk driving, but all the other charges were dropped—charges like shoplifting, drugs, and he got caught up in a sting at a gay bar for prostitution."

She stared at him. "Really? Lance? His family was wealthy."

"I know. Apparently his grandfather didn't want him in the family business, and he was an embarrassment they did their best to keep undercover."

"I can see that. They never accepted Mouse either. They were two peas in a pod. Only they came from completely opposite backgrounds. What about the guy who seduced him in the first place? I know Mouse never would let me say anything against him. But then he had a long-term relationship with him."

She watched as Laszlo tapped a notepad beside him. "He's next."

"Good. Because some guys just shouldn't get away with what they do."

"Mouse would never see it that way though."

"No, I think he actually loved him. Now whether it was sexual love, a displaced father-to-son love, I don't know. But it was definitely a twisted relationship. And like so many others in Mouse's world, I don't think he understood what a healthy relationship was at all." She watched as Laszlo stared off in the distance, his laptop open in front of him. "It's hard for you to recognize your friend in this, isn't it?"

He slid a gaze her way and nodded. "Very hard. That's not the Mouse I knew. Yes, he was definitely insecure, not terribly social, didn't do well with people in large groups and, of course, myriad other issues due to his sexuality and general lack of acceptance within the navy."

"I'm sorry. I would love it to be my Mouse. I would love to know he made it into the navy. And, if he told me that he had become a SEAL, I would be overjoyed. Because that was his dream," she said in a soft voice.

"And he deserved to have some dreams and to reach some too." He looked at her for a long moment. "If your Mouse is my Mouse, then I need to tell you that he *was* a SEAL."

She stared at him; then tears came into her eyes. She burst out crying, threw her arms around him and just hugged him close.

Instantly his arms came around to bring her closer.

She squeezed him hard, wishing she could snuggle in deep. After a moment, Minx pulled herself back. "I'm so sorry," she apologized. "I'm so sorry." With her hands waving in front of her, as if she didn't know what to do with them, she quickly retreated to her chair. She ran her fingers over her face. "I'm not normally physically demonstrative like that."

"It does show the depth of your feelings for Mouse," he said quietly.

She nodded. "And, yeah, those feelings are from a long time ago. There's no way to know if he and I would even like each other now. We were comrades in a war not of our choosing. We were helpless in a state of living we couldn't—yet—get out of. And, when he did leave, I was both bereaved and felt abandoned. I was joyous and lost at the same time." She shook her head. "It was so very difficult to come to terms with the fact that he wasn't in my life anymore.

"There was one time, months down the road, that I wondered if he'd passed. I woke up that night with this really weird feeling that I needed to go to the tree house. I slipped out of the house and crept into the backyard to climb up that tree, thinking he was there. The feeling had been so very strong, but no one was there. Still, I had to wonder." She smiled at him as she brushed away the tears. "I know that sounds like emotional hoo-ha crap. But honestly that's how I felt at the time."

"Any idea how long after he left?"

She shrugged. "I think maybe six months, but I can't be sure. It was a long time ago. But I remember standing in the tree house, realizing he wasn't there, feeling devastated all over again." She took a deep breath and sank back, picking up her hot lemon tea. "I'm a mess tonight. I'm so sorry."

"Stop apologizing," he said. "We're all entitled to our emotions. I've cried plenty in the last couple years."

She studied him over the rim of her cup. "I imagine you had darn good reason to."

He shrugged self-consciously and looked at his laptop.

"That means you're a SEAL too?" she blurted out suddenly.

He lifted his head and turned toward her. "*Former.* I'm not any longer."

"I sure hope it's my Mouse. He really wanted that."

"And yet that seems completely at odds with him being terrified of water," he said calmly. He closed his laptop and leaned back on the couch. "I can't quite reconcile that."

"Neither can I." She frowned. "It certainly seemed he was way back then, but I was a child at the time. Still Agnes says the same thing."

"Is there any chance he was either blowing it up for attention or to avoid something?"

She stared at him with a frown. "Honestly I have no idea. Like I said, he liked to make up stories."

"And you patched up his wounds after he was beaten? Enough to know he wasn't making any of that up?"

She nodded emphatically. "Absolutely. I also saw her hit him several times. Once with a chair. I wondered at that time if she didn't do some serious damage to his head. He didn't lose consciousness on me, but he didn't talk right for a couple days."

He stared at her.

She shrugged. "I tried to tell my mother about it, but she told me to leave it be."

"What did you do?"

She glared at him resentfully. "I did the only thing I

could do. I walked him to the clinic and asked them to take a look at him."

"And did they?"

She frowned and played with her bathrobe lapel. "Yes and no. I made quite a scene and a big stink. First, there was no insurance. Second, they wanted to contact his mom. But then he tried to tell them how they couldn't reach his mom, and they realized his speech was off."

"And what did they say?"

"He had a concussion. I ended up calling Agnes, and she came and got him."

"How long did he stay away?"

"Just a couple days. When he felt better, he left Agnes's and went home to his mom." Minx could see from the look on Laszlo's face that he didn't understand that kind of devotion. That kind of relationship. "I know it's hard to understand, but it was something he knew. The big world out there was something he was scared of because he didn't understand it. Neither of us were prepared for what life threw at us." There was a note of bitterness in her tone. "My boss being a good case in point. I knew that happened in my neighborhood. I didn't realize it happened everywhere."

"It happens wherever bullies get a strong-enough toehold where they feel their power and can flex their muscles." He reached for his mouse and his laptop and moved both to the coffee table. "Unfortunately it happens way more than we'd like to think."

"I can't imagine there could be someone impersonating Mouse."

"It happens, not very often," he admitted. "And it does seem far-fetched. But, at the same time, to think of someone with a panic-stricken fear of water becoming a SEAL …

We're known for all manner of water skills."

"And your Mouse was a SEAL, so he was good at that," she groaned. "There has to be an answer."

"I know. I just don't know what that answer is."

She finished her lemon tea and put the cup down. She could feel the fatigue once again pulling at her. "I think I'll try to sleep again." She stood, picked up her cup, walked to the sink, filled her cup with water and turned out the lights. "What about you?"

He shut off the living room light. "I'll try too."

She headed into her bedroom, laid her bathrobe across the foot of her bed and crawled under the covers. She could only hope she got some sleep because tomorrow was likely to be stressful at work and at the police station as well. There didn't seem to be any end to this. Yet, as she fell asleep, she was traumatized by images of Mouse's childhood. Injuries she tended, bandages she stuck on him.

Images of the times she'd tried to get her mom to help, and the times her mom had brushed her away, sometimes hitting her. It hadn't been just Mouse's life that had been difficult; hers had been too. But she'd been lucky in one sense: her mom was mostly drugged out, and it had been up to Minx to worry about making sure there was food in the house. And that hadn't been easy either, but her mother wasn't somebody to keep money hidden. As soon as she did a deal, cash was tossed on the table, and more drugs were purchased.

Any time she could, Minx had taken the money and hid it away, so she could buy food when the money got short again. Most of the time her mom would order in something, or johns would bring a meal. Sometimes Minx would get a delivery from a grocery store. But she hardly ever went out.

They had no wheels, and Minx had to take a course in high school to learn to drive. Once she started, her uncle had taken over her training. He'd been aghast at how little of the real world she understood. She didn't even have a bank account when she had moved to Maine. Or a cell phone.

He'd taken care of all those basics real fast. "You're way past the point when you should have learned about this stuff," he said quietly. "So you'll get a crash course on everything all at once."

And, true enough, he'd bought her a laptop and a cell phone. She'd been set up with a savings account and a checking account, and he even got her a credit card. And then he taught her how to use them all.

She smiled as she lay here, once again awake, thinking about her uncle. He was as good as her mom had been bad. And yet her mom hadn't been bad; she had just gone down a bad route and had never been able to crawl back out again.

Her uncle had stayed clean and had become something. He had never married, never had any kids of his own, and she liked to think he enjoyed the time she'd been there with him. He called often now and told her that she should come back and visit, but she hadn't yet. And she wondered why. There was so much unfinished business here that she didn't want to deal with. When her mom had died, her uncle had taken care of the arrangements.

He'd wanted to bring her ashes back to Maine, but, for some reason, Minx had fought the idea. Her mom had wanted to stay in Texas. Although, the Lord only knew why because she'd had a terrible life here.

Minx fell back under again. This time she saw Mouse, but, instead of his mom strangling him, he was strangling Minx. Long fingers wrapped around her neck, not giving an inch.

She woke up gasping and choking as a shadow above her was ripped away and flung hard across the room. She sat, her hands on her neck, as she realized it hadn't been a nightmare. Instead, a stranger was in her room trying to strangle her. She heard blows and thuds as the men fought outside her room. She scrambled out of bed, still gasping for air, and raced out to the living room. The last thing she wanted was for this guy to get away or to hurt Laszlo.

As she turned around, a fist came out of nowhere and clipped her in the jaw. She slammed into the wall and fell to her knees. In the dim background she could hear another fight, swearing and cussing, and then finally silence.

The silence was the scariest of all. She struggled to her feet, holding on to the wall in order to stay steady, her head pounding, her vision almost blurry. Whoever the hell had hit her had one hell of a punch. She peered around the kitchen to see someone collapsed on the floor and Laszlo struggling to get himself onto a kitchen chair.

He collapsed at the table and looked at her. "Are you okay?" His voice was low, pained.

She rushed toward him.

He held up his good hand and said, "I'm fine."

But she didn't believe him, watching as he flexed his damaged fingers. She stepped forward cautiously. "There's a cut on your forehead."

He nodded. "But everything else appears to be working."

"Your leg?"

He shot her a look, bent down and pulled up his pant leg and showed her a metal leg she hadn't taken a close look at before. Of course why would she? He'd been fully dressed. He stood up slowly and moved around the kitchen. She watched as he bent and twisted. "Have you done much fighting since you lost your leg?"

He gave her a raw grin. "Only in the gym. I used to box. I loved it. I had a wicked left, but that's the hand that was badly burned." He reached out and stretched. "It doesn't have the same impact."

"Did he know you had a prosthetic?"

"I don't know."

"But he could have known from the fight?"

"I suppose. Geir is missing his lower right leg. He hides it well."

She stared at him wordlessly. What must that be like? And how had they survived an accident that caused these horrific injuries?

As she watched, Laszlo gave himself a bit of a shake, then walked over to the unconscious man, rolled him over while she hit the light.

With the bright light shining on the man's face, she looked at him and shrugged. "I don't know him."

"Picture a full beard and a full head of hair."

She looked at Laszlo, then at the man on the floor. "Really?"

He nodded. "Really. It's the guy from the coffee shop."

"I remember when the vehicle came in, but I didn't think anything of it. I was so busy looking for a truck."

"Exactly. Create a diversion and somebody else slips in from the side."

She shuddered and stared. "Now that sucks."

LASZLO LOOKED AROUND for something to tie up his

prisoner. "Have you got some rope, something effective to tie him up? Even zip straps?"

She walked to the kitchen. "In the hardware drawer, there was a bunch that somebody was using for something."

He heard the drawer open as she pulled it out. A moment later she was back with the ties. He laced several together and quickly secured the man's hands and feet; then he did something so they were secured together.

She studied them. "That's pretty efficient. I can't get zip straps off packages when I buy them."

"Where the hell do you buy packages that have zip straps on them?"

"At the bulk-food store. They prepackage various flours and grains and put zip straps on them so they don't leak. Twist ties are never quite so secure."

He nodded. "Not a bad idea at that." Using the table, he straightened up. He hated to admit it, but whatever the hell this guy had done had set his body back at least a day. It was Laszlo's first rough fight since he'd returned from Afghanistan. There had been plenty of fighting there. He thought he was over it. But apparently not quite. He stretched, letting his body settle in again. He glanced at her. "Did you get any sleep?"

"Until I woke up with this asshole choking me, yes. Where did he come from?" She glanced at the apartment door and then the couch. "The guy would have had to walk past you. Did you not hear him?"

"No, I didn't." Laszlo walked toward her bedroom. "How does this apartment attach to the floor above?"

"It shouldn't, should it?"

"There should have been stairs originally."

There was a utility room in the back with the hot water

heater and a fuse box. She'd taken a cursory glance from the doorway, but she hadn't gone in.

When he went in, he found another door. "He came in through the upstairs."

She followed him to see the door upstairs was open. "Shit. I didn't even know that was possible."

"It also means he did know. He'd done his homework. When he could, he came in and attacked."

"Are we assuming then the man who trailed me is outside waiting for his partner?"

"It's possible." Laszlo already had his phone out, calling Geir. When the sleepy voice answered, he said, "We had an intruder. Managed to come in from an entrance we didn't know about. I caught him strangling Minx while she slept."

"Is she okay?" Geir asked, his voice harsh as he snapped fully awake. "Do you want me to come?"

"It's six o'clock. And she's fine. I have the intruder tied up. I thought maybe you'd like to join in the fun while we talk to him and see what he's up to."

"I'm on it. I'll pack up the rest of our gear and grab some coffee somewhere and then head over."

"See you in thirty then." Laszlo hung up his phone, put it into his jeans pocket and started rifling through the intruder's back pockets. He found a wallet with ID. He pulled out the driver's license, took a picture of it and sent it to Levi with a note. Then he went through the rest of the slots in the wallet. He found twenty bucks and a piece of paper with her address. He held up the sheet of paper for her to see. "Does that look familiar?"

She shook her head. "No, but it's obviously my address. So he did come here specifically for me."

He nodded. "I don't see anything else."

He flipped the intruder over and was gratified to find a cell phone. It took a bit to get it out of the unconscious man's pocket, but, when he did, he set about trying to unlock it. If it was a swipe system, then there were only so many combinations, but most people were lazy and took one of the first few options. Within a minute, he had it open. Then he sat down and checked the text messages.

"He was hired to do this. Him and his buddy. They were given the truck to tail you, and he was to follow, and, depending on where you were, try to get you between the two of them. So, while you were keeping track of the truck, you didn't notice the car. You pulled off, went into the coffee shop, the car came in behind you, but you were still so focused on the truck, you didn't notice the car. We went in. They saw us with you." He spoke as he interpreted the text messages. "And it was determined that somebody should hit you tonight. The address was given, with instructions that the upstairs of the house was not occupied and had an entrance to the downstairs suite."

"Yeah, with the owners away on vacation," she said, "it would have been an easy-enough job to go in and make himself at home, then come down during the night."

"I didn't hear anything upstairs last night. Did you?"

She shook her head. "No, it was quiet. So he must have found himself a place to crash, and then he stayed up there while we were down here and slipped in here while we were asleep."

"It would have been easy enough to have waited outside until our lights went out, give it an hour, and then gone upstairs and made his way down." He looked around the kitchen. "I don't suppose you have coffee, do you?"

"I do." She hopped up, walked over and busied herself

making a pot of coffee.

Laszlo looked down at the guy. "The question is, who hired him?"

"It doesn't say on his phone?"

"*Bill*," he said. "That's all there is in here. But I do have his number. And this guy's also got his email attached to his phone, and he has Facebook. I'll need a couple hours to go through this."

"Do we call the cops?"

"Not yet," he said absentmindedly as he started going through the phone in depth. He looked up at her. "I'll need my laptop, and we'll see if I've got a charger or some cables so I can download his contacts from this phone. Other than that, I also want his log-in information so I can go to his emails in his cell phone. And his Facebook."

She turned and looked at him. "I might have something." She went into her room and came back with a couple cables. "That's how I put music on my phone. It might work the other way too." She dropped them next to the laptop for him. "Get any information you can because, once the cops get here, you know perfectly well they'll take him and the phone."

He nodded. "Understood. You keep the coffee coming, and I'll keep this happening."

CHAPTER 10

S HE TOOK A few minutes to get changed. With Geir arriving, she didn't want to still be in her pajamas. And she knew somewhere along the line the cops would come too. She wasn't sure what kind of an excuse she was supposed to give for not having called them earlier, but nobody could dispute the timing except her and Laszlo, and she didn't get the impression he was in favor of giving the cops more information than need be. The fact that this guy was hired with his buddy to follow her was already disturbing. She wondered if Geir was on the lookout for the partner.

She stepped from the bedroom fully dressed, twisting her long reddish-brunette hair into a braid and tying off the end before flicking it down her back. "Is Geir looking for the red car?"

Laszlo nodded. "I texted him as I was getting results from the phone. He's doing a quick search outside. The best-case scenario would be if we caught the other guy too."

"I suspect he's long gone though. If this guy didn't make his rendezvous with him, then you know that guy isn't sticking around."

"But then he has to worry this guy'll talk."

"It's a simple break-and-enter charge. He'll probably get a hand slap, and the cops won't care beyond that."

"You're not a big fan of law enforcement, are you?" He

looked up, his eyes crinkling in the corners. "Something to do with that lovely childhood of yours?"

She nodded. "That's quite possible." She brought over two cups of coffee. "Any wiser?"

"These two are petty thieves. They do all kinds of break-ins. They scan houses, decide what's there, then go to the broker, tell him what they can grab, and he tells them what he wants. They go back into the house and take it."

"Why wouldn't they have taken stuff to pawn in the first place?"

"Because their broker only wants what he wants. He's quite fussy. He knows what he can sell and what he can't."

She shook her head. "It sounds like it's getting to be a high-tech business."

"It is. Your strangler also does odd jobs, like trailing people. Sometimes he works for a guy who does jobs for a couple private investigators. And that includes taking pictures of meetings, lovers, husbands cheating, things like that. He hands them over to his boss and gets paid for the photos, and the boss does whatever he's supposed to do with it."

"Well, that could just as easily be somebody who wants blackmail material and not anything about handing it over to a PI," she said. "Honestly that sounds terribly fishy."

"I think he does whatever he's asked to do, and, as long as it pays, he doesn't give a shit." He turned to glance at the guy on the floor and found him glaring at him. "Oh, look at that? You're awake. Hey, Wallace. How you doing?"

The man stayed quiet, but his glare spoke volumes.

Laszlo chuckled. "Not quite where you expected to be, huh? And what did you think I was? Just an amputee? Therefore, an easy mark?"

The man's face turned to disgust.

Laszlo nodded. "That's what I thought. But that's all right. You keep thinking that. Life often throws curves you have to react to. And you've got a mean reaction."

There was a note of admiration in Laszlo's voice she didn't understand. The man on the floor didn't say a word.

Laszlo shrugged. "Don't worry about it. I got your cell phone. I'm already going through all your shit."

"No," the man roared, trying to sit up. Because his hands and feet were tied together behind his back, it was more than awkward, and he tumbled over to the side. "Give me my phone back," he snapped.

Laszlo looked down at him and shook his head. "Hell no. This is proof you were hired to do this job. What I want to know is, who the hell is Bill?"

The man wasn't talking again.

Laszlo shrugged. "That's all right. My partner is on the way. You don't want to talk? He'll fix that."

The man shifted nervously, as if trying to free his hands.

Laszlo didn't even bother looking up. "Don't bother. You're not going anywhere."

She watched it all happen in amazement. Laszlo was so calm, and she was a wreck. She collapsed on the chair across from him, staring at the stranger. "Why me?" she cried. "I didn't do anything."

The man had the grace to drop his gaze and fall back on the floor. He wasn't talking, but he particularly wouldn't talk to her.

"Do you know if this has anything to do with my boss?" She looked at his face for some kind of recognition and then realized he probably didn't know who her boss was. When she said, "Andrew Conley," an odd look crossed the strangler's gaze, but he shook his head.

"Somebody's paying the handler—who turns around and gives these guys the low-end jobs because they aren't smart enough to do anything other than that," Laszlo said with a sneer.

She watched rage cross the man's face and realized Laszlo was trying to upset him, to get him so mad he would talk. "Is that like having a pimp?"

Laszlo chuckled. "Exactly like having a pimp. But, instead of doing sexual favors, these guys do thuggery favors."

"Thuggery." She rolled that word around. "Where the hell did you get that term from? Ancient medieval times?"

Laszlo laughed. "Well, if it fits, I don't care where it came from."

She studied him, seeing his hard edge still, yet there was also a lightness to him. He'd gotten his man, and he was damn happy with what he'd found out. She realized she was too. "Considering you've only been here for one night, you've done a hell of a job."

"Oh, it's not over yet. Wait until we get to the cops," he said. "We'll get that statement from this guy, and then we'll deal with that asshole of a boss of yours."

"What? Breaking in? You know that won't wash," she said.

"Attempted murder," he said and held up the phone.

And there in front of her was a text message that read **Take her out. Don't care how.**

She felt all the color wash away from her cheeks. "He really meant to kill me?" She turned and stared down at the man who wasn't even looking at her. And then she lost it. "You little fucker. You were going to murder me? Do you think I went through all the shit I did all my life to have some punk asshole like you cut it short?"

Laszlo reached across and grabbed her hand. Both her hands were in tight fists, and she was already standing as if ready to pummel the strangler. She turned and glared at Laszlo. "No way in hell I'll let this asshole get away with something like that."

He tugged her gently toward him, and she half fell, tripping over his leg, and ended up in his lap. "He didn't get you. If you'd been alone, he might have, but you weren't, and he didn't. We've got him now. And it doesn't matter if his partner is out there or not, because we also have his name."

She happened to be looking at the man on the floor when Laszlo said that. She watched the pinch of resignation cross his face. "Oh, now he sees how serious this is. Somebody's taken a murder-for-hire contract out on me. But instead the table has turned. This asshole gets murdered in jail. At least if there's any divine justice."

The man on the floor said, "I didn't plan on killing you."

"You were choking the life out of me pretty damn bad," she snapped. "The only other thing that probably would have been easier is to put the pillow over my face and suffocate me."

"Kind of wish I'd done that now," he said. "Probably would have been faster."

Laszlo leaned forward. "It's quite hard to strangle somebody. You're a big guy, and you've got big hands, and obviously she wouldn't offer much resistance at that point. But next time you should realize that strangling is not quite so physically easy as you might have thought."

The man nodded. "I still would've done it, if it hadn't

been for you."

"Yep, that was your intention." Laszlo nodded. "And thanks for that, by the way." Laszlo held up his phone. "Just in case you're wondering what you just said,"—he hit Play, and the man's voice filled the room. Everything they had discussed for the last ten minutes was on it, including his admission that he would have successfully choked the life out of her except for Laszlo's interference.

"So this is an open-and-shut case of attempted murder. Actually, in this case, murder for hire. So you've got at least fifteen years, if not life, coming."

He hugged Minx, who was still in his lap. "Any more of that coffee?"

She beamed, hopped up off his knee and got the coffee-pot. She gave the asshole on the floor a wide berth. "Do you think Geir has caught his partner?"

"I haven't heard from Geir, so no way to know. I did send a text to Levi, saying we now had a double need for a decent cop in town. So they could be here at any time."

"What about this guy's phone?"

Laszlo shrugged. "I've got all his log-ins. I can check his emails and his social media accounts with no problem. And I have a copy of his contacts already. They can take his phone now."

The guy on the ground roared at him. "You won't get to my partner anyway."

"It doesn't matter if we do or not. The cops can. His name is Rodney. Rodney Smyth."

The man on the floor just glared.

Laszlo nodded. "Yeah, but, if I were you, I'd start talking. I don't know how bad things could be for you in jail, and I don't understand how high up in this business world your handler is, but chances are he won't like it if you turn and talk about him. Still, you'll save your neck somewhere along the line. Otherwise, you're looking at a pretty hard sentence," Laszlo said. "And your handler would turn on you in a heartbeat, as you well know."

"No, he won't."

"Hell yeah, he will. And we'll have him picked up in no time too."

"What, because of the name Bill?" the man said in disgust. "You ain't got nothing."

"Oh, yeah. His name is Bill Fenders."

The guy's eyes widened. He started to shake his head. "Oh no, oh no, oh no."

"We will be sure to tell him how we got the information from you."

At that Minx started to laugh. For the first time in several days she started to laugh and laugh. "Oh, my God, this is priceless. Let you crooks fight it out in jail and see which one of you survives the showers. This town is so messed up. What I want to know is, will the asshole who hired Bill Fenders personally take me out?"

The guy on the floor shrugged. "Not my deal. I work with Bill, that's all."

"And that'll be enough," Laszlo said quietly. "Because we will get your partner, then we'll pick up Bill, and we'll know who's up the food chain."

At that came a knock on the door. Minx hopped to her feet, but Laszlo reached out a hand and shook his head. "His partner's still out there somewhere."

Instantly her stomach twisted in knots, and then she heard a voice.

"Laszlo, it's Geir."

Laszlo walked to the door and opened it. It was Geir, but he was with someone else.

"So you caught him."

Geir pushed another stranger into her kitchen.

She took one look and said, "He was the driver of the truck."

His hands were tied behind him, and he had a sullen look on his face. They made him lie on the floor beside his partner; then Geir and Laszlo high-fived each other.

She walked over and glared at him. "Who the hell are you, and what the hell are you doing trying to kill me?"

Neither man said a word.

"ANY TROUBLE PICKING him up?" Laszlo asked Geir.

"Hell no. Once he saw me, he realized the game was up. He came without too much fighting. I already told him that we had his partner. And, of course, this helps too." He lifted his shirt to show the handgun he carried.

He heard the gasp from Minx. But he turned and said, "Yes, we're licensed. Yes, we're used to handling them, and obviously they're very necessary right now."

She nodded, her face pale and her lips pinched. "Thank you, Geir."

He gave her a gentle smile. "You're welcome." He loudly sniffed the air. "I meant to pick up coffee, but I forgot. Is there any spare?"

She hopped up. "I'll put on a fresh pot."

As she did that, the two men sat down, and Laszlo went over what was in the first man's phone. "Let's grab the second phone and make sure we have all the information we need before the cops come."

And that's what they did. By the time they had all that taken down and stored away on Laszlo's laptop, another knock came at the door. Minx called out, "What the hell is this, Grand Central or something?"

"It'll be the cops. You sit still." Laszlo walked to the door and opened it.

Two police officers stood outside. Both held up their badges. He took them, carefully studied them, pulled out his phone and called Levi. "Did you send me somebody?"

"One should be Carson Everett. If one of them isn't, I wouldn't trust either of them," he said.

"We're in luck. One of them is Carson Everett."

Laszlo stepped back and let the cops in. Now they'd really get some action, he hoped.

CHAPTER 11

MINX WATCHED THE two cops approach warily. She didn't recognize either of them. They stopped at the entrance to the kitchen, their gazes lighting in surprise at the two men on the floor tied up. Then they stepped back to search the other rooms. She stood while they did, and their attention afterward centered and locked on her.

She smiled. "Hi. These two men stalked me, then broke into my house this morning. I woke up with this guy …" she gave him a light kick with her foot. "I woke up being strangled," she said, her hand instinctively going to her throat. "If it wasn't for Laszlo here"—she motioned at Laszlo in front of her who was still standing beside the cops—"I'd be dead."

The cops glanced at the two men on the floor and nodded. "We got a call about something like that." They turned and looked at Laszlo. "Laszlo Jensen?"

He nodded and shook their hands. "Levi tell you?"

"In a roundabout way. Detective Markham out of Houston did."

Minx watched the exchange. She didn't know any of the names mentioned, but, as long as it made this process easier, she was all for it.

"And the second man?" the second cop asked. His voice was neutral as he fished out the wallets from both men's pockets.

She was glad they'd put the wallets back in their pockets. She had wondered if the men would get to keep them or if they'd be confiscated when they went to jail. She figured it should be like a hospital, where all personal belongings were removed and kept until they were allowed back out again.

Geir picked up the story. "When I got a text from Laszlo about what had happened, I came running. We already knew of the likelihood of a second man after being at the coffee shop last night."

They interrupted him. "Did you report the stalking?"

"No, I didn't figure anybody would care," she said honestly. "And I had no way to prove it. However, Laszlo did report the stolen truck they used."

Laszlo got Carson's attention. "Did Levi tell you it was stolen?"

"Via Markham, yes. Okay, I'll have that truck checked on when we get back to the office. Which one was driving the stolen truck?"

Laszlo pointed out the second man.

"And this first guy?"

"He was driving a small red car," Minx said quietly. "I saw him in the restaurant parking lot when I was waiting in my car for Laszlo to come and rescue me from the guy who had followed me. We saw him having coffee, but then he got up and left, so I didn't think anything of it."

"Instead he was driving a second vehicle," Laszlo said. "When we left the coffee shop, the driver of the truck was gone, but the truck was still there. We'd already reported it as stolen."

"And was it still there when the cops arrived?" Geir asked the cops.

"Who knows? I'll run a trace on it and see what happened. I presume you still have the license plate, etc.?"

Laszlo repeated it. Apparently he'd memorized the number. Then he gave the model. "It was stolen five days ago."

The cops nodded. They were busy taking down notes.

At that point, one of the officers started asking her more questions, and she realized she was having her statement taken. At least she hoped so. "I'm supposed to go to the station this morning at ten to sign a statement I gave already. These two guys seem to think this is all related. I don't know that it is, but I hope so, in a way. I don't really want to think I'm up against two sets of assholes who are unrelated."

Carson glanced at her and said, "Explain."

But he didn't sound terribly surprised, so she didn't know how much back history he knew already. Still, if she was going through with this, she needed to at least make sure she told him as much as she could. Especially considering the issue had escalated. So, as clearly as she could, she explained what had happened to her up until now.

"If you talk to Officer Charter at the station," she said, "he's supposed to have my statement ready for me to sign today."

"I'm not sure if that'll happen," Carson said quietly. "He was in a car accident two days ago."

The air in the room electrified.

Laszlo stood, walked to the kitchen and leaned against the counter of the sink. "Was it an accident?"

Carson looked at him. "Without this incident, we would have thought so. But are you suggesting that potentially the same people who sent these two after her might have killed a cop or might have gone after a cop?" His voice was hard, curt, but Laszlo's nod had him swearing softly. "It's not that we don't care about what happens to you," he said by way of apology to Minx, "but to go after a cop completely changes the game. Though I'd doubt it at this point. There are enough victims connected to this killer that we don't need another one, especially a cop."

"I hope the cop is okay, but he hadn't been too helpful," she admitted. "He did, in a way, not so much as try to talk me out of filing the report, but he wanted me to be sure I was prepared to go through with this because he said it could get ugly."

"It can get ugly once you start smearing names and bringing up sexual harassment charges. But they generally aren't deadly. Although I don't know this person you're accusing. I don't even know the office where you work," Carson said. "So I can't see how any of this got so ugly this fast. It doesn't make any sense. Obviously he could face loss of pride, his job and his career, and might also cost him his life savings defending himself in court. To him, that might be enough to go to these lengths, but he's not a famous politician. He's not a huge businessman or I'd know his name and his face already."

She shook her head. "That's why I wasn't thinking this would be much of a big deal. Something else must be going on, or he just doesn't like being crossed."

"Which you already know he doesn't," Laszlo reminded her. "You got shunted off to a job in a different office entirely, basically demoted."

"He had the power to do that?" Officer Everett asked.

"He's very well-loved at the office," she said shortly. "I imagine a lot of people would do things either for him or on behalf of him."

The two cops nodded. "We'll take these two to the station and see what they say." As they brought the two men to their feet, Carson asked them, "Do you have anything to say?"

"No."

The second man just glared at them.

He nodded. "No problem."

"I'll forward the strangler's taped confession and the email with the hit ordered on Minx," Laszlo told Carson.

"Don't forget about the middleman," Geir said. "These two men were hired to do this, but there was a man in between them and whoever wanted her killed."

"And, of course, they haven't shared the handler's name?"

"The name Bill Fenders came up, but neither are talking."

"No, of course not. It's also likely a fake name. I'll get a statement written up." He glanced at his watch and shook his head. "It's probably cutting it a little too close to get it ready by the time you come down at ten this morning. But I might be able to squeeze you in, and we can get it done at the same time."

"If you could, that would be great. I'm taking a stress leave day as it is. But I won't get too many free days before it starts counting against my work record and adds to the fuel of me not deserving to have a job here at all," she said caustically.

"Understood." With that the two cops moved the two bound men forward in front of them.

Geir and Laszlo stepped in to help. They apparently wanted to make sure the cops got the men safely out of here.

Self-consciously, but needing to see the men taken away, Minx followed the group outside to the cop car and waited until they were secured in the back of the cruiser. As she stepped beside Laszlo, she asked, "Are they safe like that?"

"You notice the cops didn't untie their arms, right?"

She nodded. "I guess they can't do a whole lot then, can they?"

"No, I don't think so. The question is whether anybody's watching your place, looking for an update, and will be unhappy with these men and do something about it."

She spun and looked at him. "Are you talking about potentially taking these men out?"

"It depends. I don't know what's going on. That they would make an attempt like this surprises me. It could also be the handler interpreted the instructions in a different way. It could be a blanket statement—take care of her. Our strangler interpreted it as killing you, and these guys were going about it in their usual fashion."

"It kind of sucks that anybody can turn around and just say, *Take her out. I want to remove this problem, so make sure she doesn't come back again.* It pisses me off even more." Her voice sounded tired. "You know? Just when you think you've left the gutter, you realize the gutter never leaves you."

"Sometimes you do the best you can, and life doesn't cooperate, but that doesn't mean you give up. It's very important you keep going as planned. Walk the high road until the low road can't jump up and grab you anymore."

"I thought I had," she said quietly. "I thought I'd done everything. When I went to the cops, I did so for justice, not just for me but for the others." She shook her head. "And look what happened."

"But you're alive, and you're safe," Geir reminded her. "Although, until we get a hold of the middleman and potentially the man who placed the order, we can't guarantee there won't be a second attempt."

"I was afraid you would say that." She spun on her heels and walked back inside.

Instead of saying anything to the men as they came in, she headed straight to the bathroom and had a long hot shower. She didn't even know what to say. It was too much like having that scummy world of her childhood back again.

As she let the hot water pour over her head, she wondered if she would ever escape her history. When she was done, she stepped out and dried off. In the bedroom, she got dressed for the day. Whether she liked it or not, a new day had begun.

LASZLO WALKED BACK in behind Minx, watching as she headed to her bedroom and closed the door. He glanced around the small kitchen and then took a look at Geir. "I guess more coffee?" he asked with a laconic smile.

Geir shrugged. "Sure. But I need food."

Laszlo nodded. "So do I. Maybe when she's dressed, we'll head out to a restaurant, get breakfast, then go on to the police station." He walked to the cupboard and checked for more coffee. There was just enough to make another pot. Deciding he'd rather buy a pound of coffee for her later, as long as it meant he could have more now, he measured and set up another pot. It was a small pot, so it would give them each at least one cup, but, after that, they would find another solution.

When it was done, and they were sitting down with their laptops open, coffee beside them, he said, "It's this Bill guy we need."

"I hear you. I'm forwarding all the information we took off both cell phones to Erick. It's up to him to decide who it is who'll help us get through that information."

"It's their boss we need information on first. It almost sounds like some kind of a new industry I hadn't heard about."

Geir lifted his gaze off the laptop. "Right? I was thinking of that when we had the hit man. Because he had a middle-man as well. As if there is a boss supplying the labor—specialized labor. Hit men, thugs, safe crackers, who knows what else."

Laszlo stared at him and frowned. "Handler is the term Minx used."

The two men studied each other for a long moment. "No, of course they wouldn't be," Laszlo answered his own question. But inside he wondered. Finally he gave a shake of his head. "No, that would be foolish. At the same time, since when did this industry pop up?"

"Times are changing. Since the advent of the internet, everything's digital, everything's online, everything's anony-mous. Somebody like a handler who could pass out jobs to the right people with the right skill set, he'd be invaluable. I've heard of the dark web. I don't know how to access it, but I wonder if any of our people can?"

Laszlo shrugged but sent a quick text to Levi and Mason.

"It's a new name for the old job—middleman," Geir said. "But, because of the global world today, he could be anywhere. Chances are he's not in any Western country. He'll just have connections. As in how he found these guys."

"Unless we have two people in between. One big-time handler overseeing smaller handlers in multiple countries who all have men available."

Geir nodded. "But the more lines there are in between, the more the message gets blurred. And how would this guy, Andrew, Minx's supervisor, know how to contact anyone?"

"It sounds like he's a bit of a bully anyway. And we all know bullies know other bullies. And anybody in the criminal element, or somebody who's got that definition of what women are supposed to be used for, could easily have a reputation in the sexual world. Maybe he's used prostitutes? Maybe he's had charges against him in the past? Who knows?"

"True enough. There's got to be something. It'll take one of the criminal elements to tell us about that," Geir said. "Anybody you know?"

Laszlo settled back into his chair, thrumming his fingers on the tabletop. "I don't have any connections. Do you?"

Geir shook his head. "No. At least I don't think so."

"What does that mean?"

"I had a couple buddies in college. They were very skilled at evading the law and getting exactly what they wanted. But I don't know exactly how far down this path they went."

"We might be better off seeing if Levi has any contacts. Or Mason, for that matter. Although their contacts would be more aboveboard."

"Levi could also have someone local here. If the two men aren't talking at the station this morning, and we can't get this Bill guy to say anything, we need to find somebody in the same industry who will have a talk with us."

"In order to do that, we'll need some leverage to make them talk."

"Or you can ask Agnes," Minx said, leaning against the doorway. Her arms were across her chest, her damp hair curling and soaking into her shirt. She studied the two men. "Made yourself at home, I see."

"I'd rather buy you a new pound of coffee than do without right now," Laszlo confessed. "And sorry for taking liberties, but I wasn't sure how long you would be in there."

"Ten minutes," she said, walking over to the coffeepot. "A good thing you noticed we're out of coffee. I'd have been pissed if I woke up tomorrow, and there wasn't any."

Relieved she didn't appear bothered, he watched as she put on a second pot of coffee. The small pot was empty after one round. "What did you mean about talking to Agnes?" Laszlo asked.

"Agnes and Bart have one foot on either side of the law. They believe in it, but they help a lot of people who are on the wrong side of it. In order to help those people, they have had an awful lot of connections. It doesn't mean they'll know anybody higher up or in big business, but they might very well know where you could start."

The men nodded. "Do they serve anything else but burgers?"

She laughed. "You've never had their breakfast?" Then she shook her head. "Of course you haven't. You just arrived in town. Well, in that case, since I don't have any food, certainly not enough to feed the three of us, I suggest we go there for breakfast. You can talk to them. Then we'll head on over to the station afterward." She flipped a chair around, so she sat backward and studied both of them. "That is, if anybody is coming to the station with me?"

"I am," Laszlo said. "No way you'll keep me away."

She turned to glance at Geir. "And what will you do?"

"I'll be there, but I'll be in the background. Hopefully you'll never see me. But I'll know exactly what goes on." He gave her a slow smile. "That's my specialty."

"Being a ghost?"

He nodded approvingly. "Almost. But even ghosts have needs. And breakfast will do nicely. As long as it's not another burger."

"You didn't like the burger?" she asked. "I can't think of anyone who doesn't love them."

"I can't eat that much at one time, and heavy fat is still not something my system can handle." He stood up and excused himself, going to the washroom.

She turned an inquiring glance at Laszlo.

In a quiet voice he said, "In the accident Geir lost a large portion of his intestine, part of his stomach, his spleen and part of his liver."

Her face blanched. "I'm sorry. I keep forgetting."

"I wouldn't consider remembering something like that as anything you should do. Geir wouldn't appreciate it. But, when it comes to food, his system can't handle the same food or the same quantity as the rest of us can."

"Still, I'm sorry. He's a nice man. He's been a huge help to me. I wouldn't want him to feel uncomfortable. So we can go somewhere else if you prefer?"

"I can handle whatever Agnes throws at me for breakfast. It was one of the best burgers I've ever had. I almost got to finish off Geir's burger for him too."

"Well, if you're lucky, you'll get part of his breakfast. Their portions are huge."

"In that case I wouldn't need to eat for the rest of the day," he declared.

"Did you find anything useful while I was in the shower?"

"We're sending off the information we gathered from

the men's phones. What we're trying to do is figure out how to get information on his handler."

She nodded. "I'd say I would have known some people from the wrong side of life too, but I worked hard to get up and away from it."

"We're also trying to figure out where Lance is, see if we can talk to him."

Her gaze lifted. "Good luck with that. I haven't heard tell of him in years."

Laszlo nodded. "I haven't seen anything in the news in over seven years."

"So, either the family succeeded in hushing him up and keeping him out of trouble, or he doesn't live in the country anymore. Or he isn't alive anymore. Given his lifestyle, any of the above could be true."

"And I still haven't found the creeper, JoJo aka Poppy."

"Did you check the jails? He was a pedophile, no doubt about it."

He studied her. "You're right. I didn't even think to check on that." He sent an email to Erick, telling him about the suggestion. "I'd feel better if he was in jail. But I'm not sure anybody would have reported him."

"It's hard to say. Mouse's mother sure as hell wouldn't. Mouse wouldn't. But I doubt those were the only two people in his sick world."

"Would Lance know about him?"

"Hell yes. But I don't think they would have been close. Lance was always jealous of Poppy because Mouse talked about him in such loving terms."

Laszlo had trouble with that. He didn't care what kind of a loving relationship it was, it was hard to imagine an older man like that taking advantage of a young boy and the young boy still caring. But then that boy had been starved for love for so long, maybe anybody who reached out with a gentle caring hand looked wonderful.

Geir returned and sat back down. He tapped out another note to Erick and sent that off. "Erick will be busy all day keeping tabs on this one."

"I was thinking about that. The weapons dealer with the hidden cache in Afghanistan. We never heard from him, did we?"

"No. At least I don't think so. I don't know if Erick has though, and Erick, I think, said he would contact him."

"And what does a weapons dealer in Afghanistan have to do with this nightmare?" Minx asked. "I don't have anything to do with your problem."

Laszlo looked at her with a soft gaze. "You're so right. Somehow all of this in our heads was gelling, but you're right. Whoever was after you is not connected to us. So, these guys, even though they have a handler, won't necessarily be running in the same circle as our guys. We're just remembering loose threads we need to tie off."

"Does that mean you must return to Afghanistan?" She shook her head. "I can't say that would be anyplace I'd want to go."

"I'm not sure we have to go. We met somebody over there who thought we were after his weapons cache. We thought he had something to do with our accident. The end result was, he disappeared safely. We got out of there with our lives and with a friend who had been kidnapped and also with a woman who had been slated for delivery to a man's door for three days of fun times against her will." At Minx' soft gasp, Laszlo nodded grimly. "We've had quite the month or so. The bits of intel we've found along the way are what sent us back to Mouse. We're trying to figure out if we were targeted, but, considering only Mouse died in the accident, maybe he'd been the target. And hence we came here to start at the beginning and to see what Mouse's childhood had been like."

"And now you know," she said. "It was shit."

CHAPTER 12

I T ALL SEEMED too far-fetched for Minx. But then she knew if she tried to tell most people about her and Mouse's childhood, it would seem too far-fetched for them too. She'd mentioned it to a couple friends in college, and they thought she'd been making it up. She'd learned quickly not tell anyone anything. But then she should have known that from her childhood. Mouse had told her all the time that "You can't tell nobody nothing," and "Everyone lies, cheats and steals." He had also said, "You just got to lie better, faster and more often than the others. Keep everyone guessing."

They were in Laszlo's truck, heading toward the police station, something she was not really looking forward to. But there should have been a sense of satisfaction in knowing that the two assholes who had followed her home last night had been caught. She didn't want to think or use the phrase *the guy who strangled her* because, of course, that was a little too graphic, too close to home.

Her neck was still sore. She'd seen the bruises in the bathroom mirror this morning and had deliberately put on a scarf. If the police asked, she'd show them how the bruises were starting to come up nicely. She didn't know if they could get fingerprints or anything like that off her neck, and maybe she shouldn't have had a shower, but it never occurred to her at the time, other than to don the cheap plastic gloves to protect any DNA under her nails.

They parked and walked into the station. As soon as they explained who they were and what they were waiting for, they were asked to take a seat, and they'd be called when it was their turn. Sitting on the hard and uncomfortable wooden benches wasn't her favorite thing to do either.

"Have you ever been here before?" Laszlo asked, sitting beside her. "Outside of this issue?"

He sat close enough that they were almost touching, as if he'd done it on purpose. Protective. Letting everybody know she was his. And, if they wanted to cause trouble, they were welcome to, but they'd go through him. The possessiveness kind of went along with that protector syndrome.

She'd always been independent. … But she welcomed his actions given their early morning intruders.

But something personal was definitely blossoming between the two of them. She hadn't seen it until she had turned around, and he was just suddenly there. He was fascinating. She'd always kept her relationships a little distant. Not quite giving 100 percent of herself. She knew all too well what people did when you trusted the wrong person. They took advantage. She'd spent way too much of her life watching others hurt and take advantage of people. Another of Mouse's lessons. *Don't let anybody get too close.*

She shook her head, getting back to Laszlo's original questions. "Not in a long time. I came a couple times when Mouse got picked up for one reason or another."

"He got charged?"

She frowned. "You know? I'm not sure. He was caught shoplifting once, and the store let him off. I don't know why, but they did."

The men just sat quietly.

"Sorry we couldn't talk to Agnes this morning."

"She did tell us to come back afterward, and she'd feed us lunch."

Minx chuckled. "Are you ready for another burger?"

Laszlo grinned. "Bring it on. How they make money, I don't know."

"They're not cheap," she admitted. "But it's such good food and large portions that nobody really seems to mind."

"I imagine they mind, but they suck it up. I can't see them arguing with Agnes very much. She'd probably pick them up by the back of the shirt and belt, then heave them out of the door," Geir said with a smile.

From the tone of his voice, she couldn't help but think he admired that attitude. "You know? She probably would. I've seen her toss more than a few guys out of there."

The men looked at her.

She nodded with a big smile. "Once I was there with Mouse, and one of the guys wouldn't leave me alone. Mouse wasn't much for size back then. He was pretty skinny, had a bit of an attitude, but this guy wasn't listening to Mouse telling him to back off. I'd already told him no half a dozen times, but he wasn't taking anything the two of us said for an answer." She stopped to laugh at the memory. "Agnes came up behind him, grabbed him by the back of his collar, literally, and by his belt, while Bart held the door open for her so she could toss him out into the parking lot."

"Did he ever come back after her?"

She shook her head. "He had friends there at the time too. She told them quite clearly, if they didn't want to get barred from her place, they'd make sure that asshole stayed away from Mouse and me."

Geir's smile went up a notch.

"I never saw him again."

"Maybe he's dead," Geir said. "If you think about it, a toss like that could have busted the guy's neck."

"And then, honestly, Bart would have opened the Dumpster, and they would have tossed him in." She felt the start from both men, and she shook her head. "You've got to understand how rough my life was. There were days I woke up grateful I was even alive. Most days I just woke up hungry and grateful I was still alone in the bedroom."

Laszlo winced.

She nodded. "And the other days, I woke up grateful I wasn't Mouse. Because his days were even worse."

The men settled back.

"Hard to imagine," Laszlo said. "I grew up in Norway with a brother and a loving father and a mother who looked after us, made breakfast and saw us off to school on time. Even though I hear about such events, it still shocks me that these things occur."

"Homelessness isn't a problem in Norway, is it?"

"Not for long. The winters are too harsh. They wouldn't survive. The government is run quite differently though."

"Yeah, it's not the same in America. We might be a Western world, but we're sure as hell not as advanced as we could be."

"Understood," Geir said.

"And what's your story, Geir?"

"Don't have one. Born in the Ukraine, family immigrated to the US when I was six. We went back to the Ukraine after my father died—my mother wanted to return to her roots but she followed my father soon after, from cancer. I stayed there for the last few years of my schooling, went to college, decided that wasn't the life I wanted. I came back to America, and the rest is history."

"Is that when you guys first met each other?"

The men nodded. "We were in basic training together," Laszlo said. "Most of us were. Not all the same year, but it didn't take long for us as a unit to bond and become very close friends."

"Right. That whole togetherness thing."

Just then her name was called. She stood, and Laszlo stood with her. She glanced at Geir, expecting him to be on the other side of her, but he was already gone. Startled, she turned around, looking for him.

Laszlo tucked her arm in his and said, "Don't worry about it."

She walked after the policeman who had called her. He led the way to a desk. She sat down, and he started talking.

"Okay, so you are sure you want to move forward?"

"Not only do I want to sign it, but somebody followed me home last night from a restaurant, and then I was attacked in the early morning."

The cop's eyes widened, and he reached for a new pad of paper. "I guess we need a whole new report then too, don't we?"

"Talk to Officer Carson Everett," Laszlo said. "He's the one who came to her door this morning and took away the two men." He checked his watch. "We're supposed to meet him this morning as well."

"Two men?" He wrote down Carson's name. "I know the name, but I don't know the man. So he's handling one case, and I'm handling the other?"

"I'm pretty sure you'll find they dovetail," Laszlo said.

The cop sat back and looked at him, his gaze hard.

"What makes you say that?"

"The two men Carson picked up this morning were hired to take her out, to make sure she didn't cause any trouble. No specifics were given in their methodology."

The cop stared at him for a long moment. "Murder-for-hire?"

"Garbage disposal," Laszlo said succinctly.

Hearing it like that was horrifying. But she could understand how it made it very clear exactly what was happening.

The cop looked at her. "Is that how it was?"

She nodded. "Definitely."

"Stay here. I'll be back in a few minutes." He got up to leave the room.

She turned to look at Laszlo. "Garbage disposal?"

"It's one phrase for it. You were a problem. They wanted to get rid of you."

She slumped back in her chair and said, "Do you think it's over?"

"In what universe do you think this could possibly be over? The two guys who came after you, yeah, they've been caught. Does that stop the guy who hired them from hiring new ones? No, of course not. It depends on the depth of the order, how serious the actual man in the background is."

"I can't see Andrew doing something like that."

"Are you sure he's a nobody?"

"Didn't your friends do a search on him, tearing apart his life?"

"They're working on it, but I haven't got a report back. It's moved up the priority list, now that we've got hired killers on your case," he admitted. "But it's not exactly a five-minute process."

"I'm sorry. I know it isn't. I couldn't get that information at all. My fate would be left in the hands of the cops. I'm pretty sure that wouldn't be very good."

"I think they do their best but have only so many man-hours. So many man-hours to handle and juggle multitudes of cases."

When the officer returned, Officer Everett was beside him. She looked up at him and smiled. "Hi."

He smiled, reached over and shook their hands. "Hi. Glad to see you're looking better."

"I don't know how good I'm looking," she said, deliberately taking the scarf off her neck.

Both men's faces turned hard.

Laszlo made a strangled exclamation sound and turned her slightly so he could look at her. "I didn't see those before," he said, sounding pissed.

She held up the scarf. "I saw them when I had my shower. I put this on to stop anybody from feeling uncomfortable about them."

"Now we need to have photographs of that. I don't remember them from when I collected the men." The officer frowned at her.

"I was under a blanket because I was so cold. I wasn't thinking just how sore my throat was."

"I wish you hadn't showered. There might have been some DNA."

She held up her fingertips. "In that case you probably want to check my nails."

"But you said you had a shower."

She nodded and then with a grim smile said, "I put on plastic gloves. Just in case. After I saw the marks, although I didn't know if there was any DNA on my neck, I had tried hard to fight. I couldn't take the chance of losing anything I had scraped off my strangler. So I opened a box of hair color, pulled out the plastic gloves from inside and shoved them on."

With a nod Carson said, "Come on. Let's get you to another room, and we'll take care of that now."

They were led into a small interview room where she sat down. Within ten minutes somebody came through with a tray, scissors and some baggies. They cleaned out her nails, then cut her nails.

"I can't guarantee there is any DNA on them," she said.

"If there is, we'll find it."

After that, her neck was photographed from several different angles. When they were finally done, there was a sense of not so much relief but almost invasiveness. As if the reality had set in that it had really happened to her. She'd blocked it out until then, not wanting to see or deal with the aftermath of the attack.

As she sat here in the interview room, she said, "If that had happened when I was a child, I wouldn't have had the foresight to cover my hands during the shower. I also wouldn't have talked to the police, and I would never have given them DNA to check out."

"Not even the DNA?"

She shook her head. "Hell no. If anybody thought we had DNA on them, it wasn't worth our lives. It was one thing to be assaulted, beaten or any other number of incredibly terrible things, but, if they thought we had proof and would turn it over to the cops, our lives would be forfeit. And, when you're raised in fear, you know exactly what you have to do to stay alive. But honestly I seem to have been completely oblivious this time. I should have told Carson how I scratched him. I should have showed him my neck when he arrived."

"And I should have checked you over myself. I asked you if you were okay. You said yes, and that was it."

"And that's true," she said. "But, at the same time, I wasn't. I think I was still in shock." As a matter of fact, she wasn't very impressed with herself. She shook her head. "If I was living that life once again, thrown back into it without all these years of preparation, I'd be dead now. I've lost my edge."

LASZLO REACHED OVER and gently stroked her hand. "And maybe that's a good thing. You don't have to live in that environment anymore."

"No, but it shows my instincts are blunted. I only woke up because I couldn't breathe. If he'd put a pillow over my face, he would have killed me outright."

So much pain was in her voice that he didn't know what to say. And, to be honest, he wasn't doing very well himself. "I didn't know about the other exit. I was guarding one without realizing there was another."

"It's not your fault," she said with a head shake.

"And yet it is," he said. "Every place has to have two exits for fire safety. It never occurred to me."

"Hey, our instincts have all dulled. Two years of recovery will do that, I'm sure."

He gave her a grim look. "And yet, after the last couple weeks, I should have been back in tune with this type of work. No excuse for missing that point."

She nodded and smiled. "And yet there's only so much we can blame ourselves for."

"True enough. And it's a matter of doing better from here on in."

But inside he realized just how much guilt he felt. Having seen her bruised and discolored throat and realizing she had protected her nails so they had been cut and trimmed away with her permission, preserving any foreign DNA, well, that was smart thinking on her part but not exactly much on his. He was feeling pretty shitty about not having found the second entrance earlier.

They sat there and waited until Carson returned. He said, "Both cases are mine now."

She smiled. "Good. Maybe you'll get to close both of them."

"Hard to say. You seem pretty sure they're connected, right?"

"Unless I just happen to have shitty-enough luck that I have two assholes after me."

"Which isn't likely."

"Not in my world. I've been living relatively peacefully since I moved to my uncle's house in Maine."

"Before that?"

"I was raised by a drug-addict mother who had a rap sheet several pages long, but she's gone now."

"And did you go to juvie?"

"You'd think I would have," she said with a smile. "And, if it not for an uncle in Maine, I probably would have ended up there. But, as soon as I could, I contacted him and moved. I got out."

"And yet you came back?"

She shrugged irritably. "Yeah, that wasn't my best decision. I came back for a friend, only I ended up moving out. For a while I was worried that moving here was a mistake, but then it took a turn for the better. At least until I met my current sleazy boss. I felt like part of the reason for being here was to put my past to rest. Now the only real reason to stay is to make sure that same sleazy boss gets into trouble for what he's done."

He smiled at her sympathetically. "Hey, you did your part. Now let the cops do theirs. You don't have to move on or move away. It should be your decision and because it feels right for you now."

She smiled. "That's exactly what Laszlo has been saying."

Carson looked over at Laszlo. "And I checked on you some more."

"That should have been interesting reading," he said, his tone bland. He'd been listening to their conversation so far without contributing anything.

"It is. You have a very illustrious career."

He shrugged. "It's over. That's all that matters."

"So, are you doing some PI work now?"

"Something like that."

"And related to Levi?"

"Not by blood but by passion."

Carson seemed to understand. "He's an interesting man."

Both men dropped it. It wasn't exactly a topic Laszlo wanted to linger on. Discussing all the work Levi did wouldn't get them any further along in this case. But it did mean Carson knew Laszlo had resources. And people with skills.

"Did you check into my complaint about my boss?"

"Two men went to his office this morning. He was out. I'll stop by this afternoon, especially now that I have all these related items together. I want to have a talk with him."

"Right. What about the handler, Bill Fenders?" she asked with emphasis. "I guess you haven't had a chance to run anything down yet, have you?"

He shook his head. "No, and I just got the other files, so I'll need some time to digest what's happened so far."

"Nothing's happened." Her tone was wry. "That's why I'm asking."

"Give me at least twenty-four hours, and I'll see if I can contact your assailant. We'll go from there." He shoved the statement across the desk. "Take a moment to read this, and, if you agree with it as is, sign it, and we'll move forward."

She sat back with the paper and read it over. She held out her hand for a pen and signed the bottom. As she did so, she stood, handed it back and said, "I hope you find out something soon. Just thinking this guy might have hired men to kill me makes me a little less willing to leave it alone."

"Any idea what triggered the attack?"

She nodded. "Honestly I think it was coming here and making the complaint."

"When did you first make a complaint?"

"A month ago, to my supervisor. Like I said, I was shuffled out of the department very quickly—as in within days. Everybody told me that I was making it up, asking me how could I damage a good Christian man's career like that?"

Laszlo understood. Often those who hid behind their pious attitudes were the worst offenders. As if it gave them a shield for acting badly.

"First thing is, I'll talk to him. Then I'll talk to the rest of the staff and see if anybody knows anything."

"Good luck with that," she said with a smile. She walked toward the door and turned. "I guess there's nothing we can do but wait."

He nodded. "That's true. I promise I'll give you a call in another day or so."

She nodded and stepped outside.

Laszlo turned and said, "I presume you don't mind if we do some more digging?"

"No. Just make sure you don't cross the line," Carson said, his voice hard. "Levi has vouched for you, says you're one of the good guys, that you have a lot of skills he would like to use himself. What I don't want to have happen here is you go all vigilante. Protect her, please, because too often we get called after the fact." He tapped the file. "Last night's attack is a case in point. And go ahead and dig, see if you come up with anything. But make sure you send it my way as soon as you find out something. And, if you don't keep it legal, we don't have a case. So, like I said before, don't cross the line."

Laszlo reached out and shook his hand. "Won't be happening. I'd like to see this guy go away for a long time."

"Just make sure that *a long time* doesn't mean permanently."

Laszlo grinned. "I know the difference." He turned and walked out.

Minx waited in the hall for him. She raised a brow, inquiring, and he shrugged.

"Just the usual warning about making sure I don't interfere in police business."

She snorted. "That's hardly an issue."

"I can understand his point though," Laszlo said quietly. "What they can't do is have guys taking off and going after suspects on their own. But it won't stop me from hunting them down. If he wants to jump in at the last minute, then he can jump in. But if not"—he shrugged and gave her a grim smile—"you can bet I will."

CHAPTER 13

OUTSIDE THEY GOT into the truck. She checked her watch. "Right on schedule. It's lunchtime."

"Yeah, but it took a whole lot longer here than we expected." Yet Laszlo just sat here instead of turning on the engine.

"What are we waiting for?"

He lifted a finger and pointed down the block. "Him."

She glanced over to see Geir walking toward them. "Where did he go?"

"He was around, but he's got a very interesting ability to hide among … anything. It's not that he walks in the shadows, but he blends into groups, into people, into trees. He's very much a chameleon."

"So, you should have called him *Chameleon*."

"We tried. But it got quickly shortened to Cami, and he took great offense to that," Laszlo said with a delighted grin on his face.

Just then Geir opened the door to the truck. She slid over to the center console, and he slipped in beside her.

"I hear I'm not supposed to call you Cami," she said. The look he shot her had her gaze widening as she moved instinctively closer to Laszlo. "Whoa, okay. I was just kidding."

"Nothing is funny about that," he said quietly.

Laszlo chuckled out loud, turned on the engine and pulled the truck out into traffic. "Ready for a burger?"

"Ready to talk to Agnes," Geir confirmed. "How was the police visit?"

"They took my fingernails and pictures of my neck," she said quietly. "And apparently my first case, the sexual harassment complaint, has been handed over to Carson, so he's handling both now, as long as he can find proof that they're connected."

"He'll find it," Geir said comfortably. "It's what he does. Trust in the system."

"I want to. But I haven't found much in any government system that's worth trusting."

At that Geir let out a bark of laughter. "You got a point there."

"What about you guys? Did you find it worked in the military police or NCIS or whatever law enforcement is in your particular tribe?"

"It worked. It was often rough justice and with very little tolerance for stepping outside orders or guidelines. But it worked."

"What's one of the worst offenses?" Her gaze went from one to the other. "What would get you kicked out of the service?"

"Lots of things that you would expect, like murder, rape, etc. But one of the things most people don't think about is doing something that causes your team to lose trust in you. And that includes lying."

"Lying?"

"For example," Geir said, "one man was kicked out of the marines because he lied about falling asleep on his watch."

She stared at him in bewilderment. "So, an entire career was killed because he fell asleep?"

"Not just fell asleep though," Laszlo continued the story. "When he was asked if he'd fallen asleep, he lied. He said no. He was given one more chance to tell the truth, and he still said no, said he hadn't fallen asleep. But, once faced with proof that he had fallen asleep, he capitulated and admitted it."

She sat here in confusion. "I don't get it."

"He was kicked out not so much because he'd lied and not so much because he'd fallen asleep, but because, when he was given that chance to step up and admit what he'd done, he didn't. And that meant nobody could trust him. And, in our world, trust is everything."

She digested that for several moments. "That would have been very hard for Mouse."

They looked at her in surprise.

Geir asked, "Why?"

"Because Mouse always said you had to be the bigger, better, fastest liar in order to survive in this world." She caught the strange silence in the cab. "And we're back again to thinking my Mouse can't be your Mouse." She shook her head. "I just don't get it. The man you're talking about is not the boy I knew."

"Maybe that's a good thing," Geir said. "Think about it. That boy was abused, learned to lie, cheat, steal—I presume, since he was caught shoplifting. The man we knew was honest, capable, durable. He took whatever was thrown at him, and he kept on going."

"Mouse had that adaptability," she said slowly. "He did take whatever was thrown at him, and he did bend to the wind. And he always managed to stand back up again. But he swore that the only way to survive in life was by cheating and stealing, but particularly by lying." She glanced at each of them. "Have you ever considered the Mouse you knew was living a big lie? That, even if he was my Mouse, between being my Mouse and your Mouse, he was something else, someone else?"

This time the silence went on even longer.

She nodded. "It just occurred to me, as we're dissecting these two personas of the same man, maybe there's a third one as well. One that bridges the gap between them." She looked at Laszlo, then Geir. "When did he become a SEAL? When did you guys first meet him?"

"Only a year before our accident," Geir said, his voice thoughtful. "He was the youngest of all of us."

"And that's a very interesting concept," Laszlo said. "Maybe it wasn't two separate Mouses. Maybe it was one person, playing three versions of Mouse."

"But that would imply that each iteration of who he was, was just as powerful as the first," Geir said. "We've certainly seen personalities change, grow, become something else. And sometimes morph into something very different than what they first started out being."

"Exactly," she said. "So, the question really is, what would it take for the child Mouse to turn into the man Mouse who would then turn into being the Mouse you knew?"

"Whatever it was, maybe we should be thanking him," Laszlo said. "Because the Mouse we knew was a good man."

She wanted to believe that. She really did. At the same time, she just wasn't so sure. Because what if the man they knew was just a sneakier, cleverer, more brilliant man version of what she knew as a child?

LASZLO DROVE INTO the parking lot to find Agnes's place completely packed. He shook his head. "Okay, so this might explain how they stay in business."

"Drive around to the back," Minx said quietly. "There's usually parking back there for one of us deemed as special customers."

Sure enough, they drove around to the very back, and between two vehicles was a spot. He pulled into it carefully as it wasn't very big. "Do they keep it for you?"

"I'm only one of easily thirty people they keep it open for."

"That many?" Geir asked.

"It could be twice that by now. I was gone for a lot of years. But every time I come around here, it's been empty."

"Good." Geir hopped out, the others doing the same.

As they walked into the restaurant, Laszlo realized the parking lot was indicative of the table situation. "There isn't any place to sit."

But she walked ahead of them without a care, sitting at the bar. There were three stools. But it wasn't private.

As they sat down on either side of her, Laszlo said, "Hardly a way to talk."

"I know, but a table will clear eventually, and we can take it then."

Agnes came over and gave each of them an intense look. But she wrapped an arm around Minx until she caught sight of her throat. Her voice deepened as she snapped, "Did you catch that asshole?"

Minx opened her arms and stepped into a nice big hug from Agnes. "Laszlo did."

Agnes looked at Laszlo, but he shrugged self-consciously and accepted a cup of coffee from Bart. Agnes stepped back, reached around with one arm, and, with a long squeeze, she hugged Laszlo too. "Thank you."

Laszlo heard such a deep-felt emotion in her voice. As he glanced at Minx, her eyes glistened. "Maybe this is why Minx came back home. Because you were somebody who cared for Minx," Laszlo said to Agnes.

When Minx felt the tears burning the corner of her eyes, she quickly wiped them away and said, "Geir found the second guy."

Agnes's gaze turned to her. "Two of them?"

Minx nodded. "Both the men were at the coffee shop I ran to after calling Laszlo, and they followed me home."

Agnes looked around, took one look at Geir and said, "Thank you."

Geir, much to Minx's amusement, made a similar shoulder shrug, a self-conscious reaction to the affection or the accolade.

"We'll get you some food really quick. And then I want to hear the details."

Realizing she had forgotten to put her scarf back around her neck, Laszlo picked up her scarf and held it out to her. She quickly arranged it to hide the worst of the marks on her throat before the rest of the crowd noticed. He understood she wasn't the kind to attract attention. The problem was, she was damn pretty. But then, with her upbringing, she'd probably developed a second sense of trouble following any undue attention. *Same for Mouse.*

As if mirroring his thoughts, she said, "The thing about Mouse, he was very streetwise."

"And?" Laszlo asked.

"Whatever it is that happened to him, he should have seen it coming. He was very aware that way."

"But he was also looking to be loved," Geir said. "So, if somebody in his inner circle turned around and betrayed him, that's a different story altogether."

"I hope it wasn't. But you're right. He was looking to be loved. Whether that was sexual, romantic or on a friendship level."

"We need to have a talk with Lance."

"Sure, but like I said, he disappeared off the face of the earth, so chances are that won't happen."

"But that doesn't change the fact that sex is the easiest way to get under somebody's skin." Geir took a sip of his coffee and continued. "Sex is the easiest way to get close to a person and to get through their defenses."

"I get that, but I'd sure hate for that to have happened to him."

"It already did once," Laszlo said. "A pedophile out there has a lot to answer for."

"And yet we still don't have any answers."

Laszlo pulled out his phone and checked his messages. "Nothing yet."

It was frustrating. They'd sent in a ton of information, but they weren't getting much back in response to that added intel. But then he had no way to know what was going on in Erick's world either. On the off-chance he might get some response with another reminder, he sent a quick text message, saying, **Any news?**

The answer came back quickly. **No. Still working on it. No sign of the pedophile. No sign of your Lance dude. We're getting backgrounds on both men. And we have a persona made up on the handler. But zero history. As if**

it was just created for the job.

Laszlo quickly relayed that information to the other two. Both shook their heads in disgust. "In other words, he's been doing it for a while."

"Exactly."

"And you said something about an Afghanistan link?"

"No, that was with our original problem. But we still haven't heard anything from him either."

She looked confused, and he wanted to leave it that way. Enough was going on right now without adding all that mess to it. But he exchanged glances with Geir and saw the question in his eyes. He shook his head.

Laszlo sent another message to Erick. **Anything else coming out of the weapons dealer?**

I'll ask Ice and Tesla.

Laszlo leaned forward and said to Geir, "He'll check if there was anything on that bug we planted."

"Right. Well, at least there's that little bit. What we should have done was gotten an easy way to communicate with that rebel leader," he said. "At least then we'd have a way to follow-up on whether somebody in his own army was bad news."

Laszlo's phone rang, and he answered it. "Erick, what's up?"

"Just talked to Tesla. She got something out of the bug we left at the arms dealer in Afghanistan. She's been trying to run it through translators and confirm the intel. But it looks like the weapons dealer's number one supplier—the rebel leader we met in Kabul—went through a cleaning up of his house. A large grave was found with ten bodies—all suspected to be his men."

"Ten?"

"Which, if you think about it, our little guy could easily have been setting up his own minor army to take over the big guys. You know for a fact that, every time you gain power, you watch out for those below you coming to knock you off."

"Right. But there's no way to know how or why, or whether it's the asshole we're thinking of."

"The arms dealer is nervous. He knows some of the men who died, but he's not sure why they were taken down or by who exactly."

"Presumably because they were trying to overthrow the rebel leader, the boss man in charge of that area."

"Exactly."

"Can we confirm who was killed? Is it the buyer, the man who set up the mine?"

"No. But we've got somebody over there that's on it."

"Keep me in the loop." He hung up the phone.

Just then Bart arrived with large platters of fries and burgers. Laszlo stared at them in delight. "I don't know how you do it, but these burgers are dynamite."

And true to style, a salad arrived in front of Minx. Laszlo glanced over at the supersized burger plate with fries and her second plate with the salad. "Are you going to eat it all?"

She chuckled. "Watch me."

To his amazement she did. But Geir once again couldn't finish his fries, although, by the time Laszlo was almost done with his own, he wasn't sure he could help Geir out either. With multiple pots of coffee sloshing through his system, the food settled in nicely. Now what they needed to do was talk to Agnes. And that would mean waiting until the rush was over. And so they did.

They finally moved to a table in the back, and, with only

one table in the front still occupied, Agnes sat down beside them. "What's the matter?"

"We're looking for a handler," Laszlo said quietly. "The two men who attacked Minx were hired, but there was a middleman. And this handler is someone these two men have worked with for years."

She leaned forward as she thrummed her fingers on the table. "And you want to know who he is?"

"Do you know who he is? The only name we got was Bill Fenders."

"It's not his real name." Agnes glanced over at Minx. "You know him too."

She raised her eyebrows. "I do?"

"You do."

Minx shook her head. "I don't have any connections anymore to that life."

"I didn't say a connection. But you'll know the handler. He didn't start that way. He went underground, and he stayed underground."

"Who is he?"

Agnes glanced around, but nobody was here now. Then she said, "He was very close to Mouse."

Laszlo's gut clenched. In a soft tone he said, "Lance Smithson?"

Agnes nodded. "Bingo."

"In other words, he's so far underground that he doesn't care anymore? He knows he won't get caught." Laszlo leaned forward. "But why would he let anybody go after Minx?"

"A couple reasons. Lance hated Minx because she tried to break them up."

Minx yelped, "I did not."

"You didn't want Mouse to leave."

"Of course I didn't. He was leaving me."

Agnes nodded. "Exactly. And, at the same time, Lance was somebody who, if you paid him enough money, he'd do anything. And I mean *anything*. So not the best influence over Mouse and the two of them together were bad news."

Laszlo glanced at Minx's face and realized how much of this was news to her. But then she'd been a young child, barely a teenager.

"And that's why nothing's showing up in the news about him or from his family. And the name?"

"It's fake," Agnes said. "His family has cut him off, completely disowned him. He's changed his name, pretty well everything about his life. But, every once in a while, he still gets a hankering for Bart's burgers. He comes in here. But he never comes in alone."

"Can you set up a meet?"

Agnes frowned, her body stilling as she settled back farther into the chair.

Laszlo was afraid the chair wouldn't be strong enough to hold her bulk.

She shook her head. "It wouldn't be a good idea."

"Why?"

"For one, I don't get in the middle of anything. I don't take sides, and that's the way me and Bart stay alive. But, for another, he'll want to show you who he is, or what he does, and he sure as hell won't tell you anything. And our history has shown us that, a lot of times when somebody fails, their neck is on the chopping block. Lance has a good name in his particular industry. If he fails, he'll get a second chance. If he fails in that second chance, then he could be in trouble." She stared off at the blank wall, her expression hard. "I don't like anything about this."

Minx said from across the table, "That just means he'll send more people after me."

"Unless he cancels the contract," Geir noted.

"Not going to happen. And it won't make a difference," Agnes added. "Whoever is paying the handler will just find somebody else."

"What would it take for Lance to give up the name of the guy with the contract?"

"Immunity and lots of money," Agnes said succinctly.

"I don't have lots of money," Minx said. "Neither do I want to prosecute him. I want the guy above him."

"Of course you do. The trouble is, Lance won't take a chance on that." Agnes shook her head. "It's certainly not in our best interests to get in the middle of this. Especially not if we want to stay out of trouble." She shrugged. "Just sit here for a minute." She heaved her bulk off the chair and headed to the back room.

Laszlo reached across and covered Minx's hands. She had gripped them together so tight they were almost white. When he peeled her fingers apart, he realized she'd cut crescent-moon-shaped slices into her palms.

She stared down at them and shuddered. "I didn't like Lance. And I was terribly jealous. I was terrified of being alone, so I didn't want Mouse to leave. But it's not like anything I said made a difference. He did leave. He left with Lance."

"In other words, Lance not only has information about Mouse," Laszlo said, "he also knows who put out the hit on you."

She lifted her gaze, and he could see the agony inside her eyes.

"I don't like where any of this is going," she said. "I really tried to leave it all behind."

"I don't doubt you did," he said quietly. "But too often this shit just never lets go."

She pulled her hands free from his and slid back in her chair. "I don't even know what to do now."

"Let's see what Agnes says first," Geir said. "I understand her position. She needs to keep her and Bart safe, but she would also want to keep you safe too. Plus she has information we need. She has a contact we need to make."

Bart walked over then and bent down toward them. "I just sent a message. We'll see what he says." He slid on past with a big cloth in his hand, wiping the tables behind them.

Laszlo and Geir exchanged glances. "How long are we supposed to wait?" Geir asked.

"We can leave," Minx said wearily. "Chances are it'll take forever."

They got up, and she grabbed her purse, throwing it over her shoulder.

Laszlo stepped up behind her to walk her to the door, but Agnes called out, "Minx?"

Minx turned to look at her.

Agnes waved her hand. "Come over here please."

With a last glance over at Bart, Minx walked toward Agnes.

In a voice too low to be heard easily, Agnes said, "He says he'll talk to you but only you."

CHAPTER 14

MINX SAT ON the park bench not understanding how her world had shifted so fast. Nobody was around, but she knew Laszlo and Geir were hidden somewhere close. She also wore a wire, even though where the hell they got shit like that when they'd only been here for a day or two, she didn't know. But they wanted to make sure they knew exactly what was said. She had yet another cup of coffee in her hand. Mostly for the warmth because inside she was quaking and shaking with cold. The last thing she wanted was to see Lance. He hadn't been her favorite person in the first place. But to know he'd facilitated a hit on her and was to meet with her meant he could be coming with a knife to take her out personally.

Just as she worked herself up into a lather, a man sat down at the far end of the bench. "Long time no see," he said.

She glanced over and started. "I wouldn't have recognized you."

"Nope, nobody does," he said generally. "That's what makes it work so well."

"And yet you accepted a hit to take me out?"

"It's good money." He shrugged, completely disinterested in who she was.

"I never hated you, you know? I wanted Mouse to stay,

but that's because I was a scared kid, and he was the closest friend I had."

"Whatever."

"The least you could do is tell me how to get out of this."

"You started it when you went to the cops about Andrew Conley."

"Do you have any idea how he treats his employees? What he does? What he demands in order to keep your job?"

"Not my problem."

"I see. So, as long as somebody's got the money, you just send out the hit, is that it?"

"That's it."

"What happens now that your men failed?"

"Not an issue. I've got more men." But an edge had entered his voice.

Inside she felt such pain and confusion she didn't know what to do. "And what am I supposed to do with that?"

"Run?" He cackled. "Mouse always said you didn't have the smarts to make it on the street."

That was almost a visceral hit. "Really?"

He nodded. "He said you were too innocent, too naive. You were too trusting."

She thought about that. "Compared to him, maybe. But you took off with him."

"Not for long. He ditched me soon after."

"Really?" Something in his voice made her wonder. "Is that why you hate me so much? Because you were taken in by him too?"

He gave her a hard glare. "I wasn't taken in. I was happy when he left."

But she saw it in his eyes. She shook her head. "No, you

loved him as much as I did."

"Not likely," he said. "Besides life is different now."

She nodded. "It so is. But I still don't know what happened to him."

"He decided he liked Poppy better."

She winced. "He stayed with that molester?"

"And you know that he would have told you off if he heard you call him that."

"I know. I did once."

"But, yeah, the pedophile."

"Hell," she said in disgust. "Then he probably ended up in some ditch somewhere, discarded by him too."

"Nope, not at all."

She stared at him. "Have you seen him since?"

"Nope. He reinvented himself. Just like I did. That's the one thing the year we did spend together showed us. How to discard the old and create the new."

"You came from such high beginnings," she said. "Why would you want to be who you are now?"

He chuckled. "You see? You would never understand. It's not even the money. It's all about power. And growing up, living the life I lived, I had none. If I'd stayed where I was, I would never have had any. My grandfather is still alive. And then there's my father and my younger brother. They all have the power. I had none," he said cheerfully. "So I decided to change that. And now I have power."

"And you have nothing to do with your family?"

"Not yet. I'm biding my time. Haven't figured out my move, but, at some point, I'll make a change," he said with a sneer.

"And take out all your family? Really?"

He gave her a flat stare. "What do you care? Your life's

in jeopardy now."

She nodded. "It is, and I want to fix that."

"The contract is open. I've already been instructed to make sure two more men are sent out."

"And have you sent them already?" she asked, dread in her stomach. She tried to keep her voice neutral, but it was hard seeing the reality of somebody she knew as a child, somebody who had been idealistic and so in love with Mouse, somebody who'd come from Easy Street and had loved to slum it with them in their corner of the world. She just didn't understand it and didn't understand how he could choose this life over that one.

"I haven't yet," he said. "When Agnes called me, I figured this was too much fun to pass up. Besides, a walk down memory lane just reminds me of how much I hated you. Maybe I'll send three men after you and make sure they rough you up first."

She shook inside but hadn't been raised the way she'd been raised for nothing. "And you might find yourself surprised at the reception they get," she said. "Two went down. How many men have you got?"

He laughed out loud. "There are so many out there, I will never run out."

She thought about that. "What if something happens to you?"

"I'm sure somebody else will take my place," he said with another laugh. "But it's not going to happen."

"This asshole who put out the contract on me, he'll talk. You know that, right? He's one of those big blustery assholes, and he's all about power too. But his idea of power is over helpless women. He doesn't give a shit about anybody else."

"Yeah, I was thinking about that. He's definitely a problem. He's making lots of noise about you, and, if there's one thing that's golden in my world, it's silence."

"So, what? You take the hit, get the money, and then turn around and take him out?"

He glanced at her. "You want to hire me to do that?"

"And why would I do that, when the only way you'll get paid by him is if I'm dead?"

He studied her for a long moment. "Besides, you don't have the money."

"Even if I did have the money, why would I pay you to take out somebody after I'm dead?" she asked drily. "Especially if you won't take money to call off the hit."

"Well, the only way I'll be able to call it off is if I take him out, so essentially you'd be putting out a hit on him. The question is, which one gets fulfilled first."

This was the most bizarre conversation she'd ever had. She didn't know what to make of it. She shook her head. "It still doesn't change the fact I want to live."

"Then you got a problem on your hands. Talk to the two men you're with. Maybe they'll have a solution." He grinned at her and stood. "And, if you think I didn't know about them, you're a fool. But then I already knew you were a fool. Because, of all the things I could trust about Mouse, he knew people. He could spot them a mile away. I don't know where your two goons are, but you should know I've got at least four with me."

She wondered at that. "And so that's it? I better watch my back, and you'll keep throwing men at me until one of them finally succeeds?"

"That's not what I said, is it? I said, *talk to your goons*," he snapped. "If you managed to pick people a whole lot smarter than you, they might have a reasonable answer here.

Otherwise, yeah, that's probably what'll happen." He got up and walked away.

Just before he was out of earshot she called after him. "Is Mouse still alive?"

He spun around, looked at her and shrugged. "I doubt it. He lived a risky lifestyle in a big city. Not sure that pedophile really gave a damn about him really."

"Do you know who the pedophile was?" she asked as an afterthought. They had one name, but confirmation would be helpful.

He laughed. "Why? You want to sell him a little boy? Because he's not into girls, you know."

"I know," she said starkly. "He came after me once, and Mouse clipped him on the jaw for it."

Lance stopped and stared at her. "Really?"

She nodded. "I don't think he was after me sexually. I think he was upset at the relationship Mouse and I had."

Lance stood with his hands in his jeans pockets for a long moment and nodded. "That actually makes sense. Mouse was very much on your side. Nobody was allowed to hurt you. The trouble was, he also let himself be the beating stick others could tear up instead of you. And he liked that part."

"He liked what part?" she asked, confused.

He chuckled. "You're such an innocent. He liked pain. Mouse liked pain." And he turned and walked away.

Minx watched as Lance walked toward the woods on the other side of the parking lot. She could see shadows moving in the trees. But were they his men or her own? Not that she could call Laszlo and Geir *her* men. But she was grateful they were on her side. It pissed her off that Lance had the information she needed—not just needed, desperately needed. And that he wasn't willing to call off the contract. He didn't give a shit that he knew her. He didn't give a shit about their history. If anything, he'd probably laughed when he took the contract. At the same time, she couldn't let him get away with it.

"Hey, Lance," she yelled.

He lifted a hand with a finger straight up in the air.

"I wouldn't do that if I were you."

He slowed, turned to look at her, and she watched as Laszlo came out of the trees and cold-cocked him, a hard hit that knocked him to the ground.

She gasped and raced toward him. "Oh, my God! Did you just kill him?"

Laszlo snorted. "Like hell I did. We'll have a talk with Lance, and we'll get this sorted out right now."

"And how do you propose to do that?" she snapped. "I already asked him. He won't help." She spun around, remembering what Lance had said about his men. "What about his men? Are we in danger here?"

"I took out one. Geir is on the other two."

"He came with three? He said he came with at least four."

"He lied."

She snorted. "Of course he did. That would be so him. Where do you want to take him?"

She watched as Laszlo tied Lance's hands and checked him for weapons. He pulled out a handgun and stuck it into his belt, then he quickly pulled out Lance's wallet and his cell phone. He dragged Lance out of the path and set him down on a rock, leaning against the tree. To any passerby it looked like he was sitting here, enjoying the outdoors.

Laszlo quickly went through Lance's wallet, checked his

name, found several business cards, which he removed. He did the same for the credit cards. He laid them down on another rock and took photos of everything. Then he put everything together and popped it all back into his wallet, returning it to his pocket. But he held up the cell phone.

She looked at him. "Can you download the information?"

"I can get some of it. But, without a laptop, I can't get it all."

Just then Geir sidled through the trees. She stared at him. "You're absolutely freaky. I never see you coming and going."

He sent her a brief look. "You're not supposed to." In his hand was a laptop.

Laszlo nodded. "Let's do this."

She watched the men handle two phones and a cable, doing something between them. "Already done?"

Laszlo nodded. "You keep an eye on this guy. If he wakes up, he'll try to get away. And he's dangerous, even tied up like this."

Instinctively she stepped back.

Laszlo nodded. "Smart."

Geir placed a hand to Lance's neck, then nodded to himself.

She assumed that meant he was still breathing. With the two men sitting down beside Lance, they turned on the laptop, now connecting Lance's phone to it via the cable, and started downloading information.

"Can you guys get all his texts and messages off there?"

"It would be hard to get everything. But he has a memory chip. And that we are so going to take." He showed it to her and quickly pocketed it. "We'll transfer everything to the laptop as soon as Geir is done. But I don't want him getting his phone back without us knowing what's on it."

Just then they heard a moan come from Lance. She took a step back while Laszlo placed a hand on Lance's neck and shoulder region. She couldn't see what he was doing, but she could hear Lance cry out.

LASZLO LOWERED HIMSELF slightly and whispered into Lance's ear, "I'm the guy you should be worried about." His voice was dark and hard. "Because you sent men after Minx. Now I want to know the name of the man who's got the contract, or I'll drop you at the police station and put the word on the street that you've turned tail." He'd heard what Lance had said to Minx, but he also wanted it recorded.

Lance's gaze was wide and black with hate. "You wouldn't fucking dare," he roared.

Geir reached over, and Lance froze. Minx took another step back.

Lance started speaking. "You know, if you do that, my life is forfeit."

"Why do I give a shit?" Laszlo said carelessly. "You already forfeited Minx's life."

"That bitch," Lance snarled. "Mouse did anything for her."

"That's because she was the kid sister he never had," Geir said. "What the hell were you, just a jealous boyfriend?"

"Life was rough back then," Lance said. "I'd have done anything to have had Mouse's attention."

"You did have his attention," Laszlo said. "He left with you, for God's sake, leaving Minx to fend for herself at the age of fourteen."

"Yeah, but he wasn't happy with just me. Once he got a taste of freedom, Mouse wanted it all. He wanted power almost as bad as I did. We were becoming very competitive about it. We chose different paths."

"Well, you went into the streets and became a thug," Geir said with a sneer. "What the hell path did Mouse take?"

"He went in a similar direction. But he had bigger dreams. He had techno guts and brains. I didn't have any of that. I had brawn, and I knew how to make men happy," Lance said. "I got into a network, drug smuggling, prostitution. But I wouldn't stay on the bottom. I moved my way up very quickly. Now it's my network, and I created a specialty for myself. *Information.* I buy and sell secrets. I take care of people. I do jobs that need to be done. Of course I don't dirty my own hands. I hire other people."

"Until those people turn and talk to the police," Geir said.

"They know better than that," Lance said confidently. "They would never have talked."

"Well, they're in the police station. And you're here," Laszlo said.

"Yeah, but you're not cops," Lance said. "I don't know what your stake is in this. I don't know how much she's paying you, but, with your kind of skills, I can put you to work anytime you want. Just say the word."

Minx gasped. "Why? So you can take my bodyguards away from me? Hire them to do more of your dirty shit?"

Lance shrugged. "You want something from me. Why the hell shouldn't I?"

"We'll get what we want from you. We want to know who put out the hit on her. And my threat is real." Laszlo stepped back and looked down at him. "Just in case you think I'm joking ..."

That same beady-eyed hate beamed out of Lance's eyes. "I know assholes like you. You think you're so full of honor and righteousness. But you're nothing more than a thug, just like me. The same under the skin."

Laszlo shook his head very slowly. "We're nothing alike. I'd never kill anybody who didn't deserve killing. But I can see you do deserve killing."

Lance shrugged. "My guys are here."

"Nope, your guys *were* here," Geir said. "But they aren't any longer."

Lance looked at him. "Are they alive?" His words were harsh. And then he appeared to be unconcerned as he relaxed back against the tree. "Doesn't matter if they are or they aren't because I'll just replace them."

"They're down at the police station by now," Geir said.

Lance froze. "What the fuck?"

Geir turned to look at him. "Everybody has a weak spot. You just have to know how to apply pressure to that spot."

"And what's that mean?" Lance sneered.

"*Face*," Laszlo said quietly. "You don't want to lose face. Your power is all about standing behind your brand. And your brand says, you can get it done. Doesn't matter what it is, where it is, or how tough."

Lance nodded. "Very good."

"Which means, all we have to do is let everybody know you've turned. That you lost your brand because you failed. And you lied to your suppliers, and you lied to the contractor. And you turned it all into the cops because you're dirty."

Lance shook his head, but she could see the panic developing on his face.

"You can't do that. I'll be ruined."

"Not only ruined, you'll be on the run," Geir said. He turned off the laptop, closed it and stood. "So we have a couple things we need from you. First off, we want to know who the asshole is, and I want it on tape exactly what he's done and how much he's paying you to get rid of Minx. And then I want to know what the hell you know about Mouse."

He shook his head. "I'll tell you one. But I sure as hell ain't telling you the other."

"Then tell us the one you think you'll tell us." Laszlo held up a recorder and hit Play. "Anytime now, Lance. Keep talking."

Lance glared at him. "Okay, fine. It's that stupid asshole she works for. Or worked for. He's got a high deal going. Property investor with a daughter. He's trying desperately to snag the daughter in marriage and knows that any talk about him and sexual harassment and trying to get the women to service him for his own needs at work will blow it all up in his face."

"Names, dates, times?"

Lance readily filled in the details. Laszlo glanced over at Minx. "Anything else you want to know?"

She stared at Lance with her jaw open. "That little weasel."

Lance laughed. "He loves you too, sweetheart."

As soon as that was done, Geir looked at Laszlo. Laszlo looked at Geir. And Laszlo grabbed Minx by the hand. "You and I are going to the truck." But they stood there for a moment.

Lance smiled. "Bye-bye, sweetie."

Only then did he realize Geir wasn't going anywhere.

"Hey, no, no, no. Don't leave me with him, dude.

This … this dude is scary," Lance yelped.

Minx scrunched up her face while Laszlo wrapped an arm around her shoulders.

"I'm not going anywhere." Geir's smile was enough to scare anyone, and Lance shuddered, making Laszlo even happier.

"We need to know everything there is to know about Mouse," Geir said softly. Too softly.

Minx must have wondered too what else Lance could tell them about Mouse. She studied Laszlo, then spoke to the man on the rock. "Lance, you better tell him. I know these two. You'll be crow bait by the time they're done."

He stared at her, shock in his eyes, then his gaze went from one man to the other. "What the fuck do you want to know? There's nothing else I can tell you."

"I want to know exactly where you went, who you went with, from the time you left town with Mouse, and I want to know when you parted ways with Mouse, and if you've heard from him since."

"We stayed together for a year, that's it. But he wouldn't give up his bloody Poppy, the pedophile. He figured that guy would take him far. And he knew how to make him happy."

"Why would he think that?"

"Because he was ex-military. He was an ex-navy SEAL or some stupid thing," Lance spat. "And that's what Mouse always wanted to be. And this guy was it, the real thing. Mouse idolized him. He believed everything Poppy said. Poppy worked at Coronado for a while. At least that's what I heard. But he wasn't active anymore. He got injured, and he was sidelined."

Laszlo didn't know if he believed him. "Keep talking."

"What the hell? We went to California. We went to Coronado. Mouse hung around the base, tried to find somebody there who would make life easier for him because Poppy couldn't get any of his connections to get Mouse in for a long time and for a lot of money. In the meantime, when it looked like Mouse might make it into the SEALs, he started to puff up like a rooster. He got really macho. Very un-Mouse-like. But he kept running home to Poppy. Anything to keep Poppy working to make Mouse's dreams come true. And Mouse finally succeeded."

"And what was Poppy doing for him?"

"Outside of filling his head full of dreams and getting him into the military, I don't know," Lance said, "because it was still the bottom line. Mouse hated water. And Poppy knew it. But he'd do anything to keep Mouse at his side."

"Including forging documents?" Geir said slowly, standing up. He glanced over at Laszlo. "Remember that scandal hushed up really quickly a few years back? They caught a couple servicemen with fake IDs. And, when they were done, six people were kicked out of the service. I don't think they ever caught whoever was behind it."

Laszlo racked his brains, thinking about it. "So, what? Mouse just skipped all his training, and he's all of a sudden in the navy?" He was horrified to even consider that.

"Well, that's what happened to the others. But most of them were land-based. They were supply clerks, etc.," Geir said. "I remember knowing somebody involved in that." He frowned. "I can't remember who it was. But Mason will know. Mason and Tesla will know exactly who I'm talking about."

Laszlo stared at Lance. "How afraid of water was Mouse?"

"I would have thought he was terrified, but you see? The thing about Mouse is, you never really knew where you stood with him. He was a liar. He was a cheat, but he was ever-so-sweet in bed." Lance stared moodily at the ground. "I loved the man. Like, I really loved him."

Geir stepped back. "Anything else?"

"I don't think so. We did everything together, except for the days he was with Poppy. Find Poppy, and you should be able to find Mouse." He nodded toward his hands. "You want to untie me now? I need to find out if there's anything left of my organization."

"I will, but I don't want you accepting murder contracts anymore."

Lance just looked at him.

Laszlo smiled. "If you think we won't hear, you're wrong." He motioned to Geir. "Let's pack it up and go home."

Lance called out to him. "I'll be sure to put the word out to the interested parties that you're asking about Mouse."

Geir laughed, but he didn't turn back. "No one gives a shit."

Just then a hard crack resounded through the air. Laszlo dropped to the ground, pulling Minx with him. In the eerie silence afterward, he rolled over, pulling her with him behind a tree. Geir was already up and running through the trees. But it was too late. Like they'd been too late at every stage of this ugly game so far. Laszlo held Minx close in his arms.

She was shaking. "Who was that?" she whispered.

"It could be one of several men," he said. "From your old boss who put out the contract to someone in Lance's own downline who thought this was a perfect opportunity to move up the line or even the asshole I'm after. The police will find out—eventually."

Minutes later Geir slipped around beside him. "Executed. Clean shot, center of the forehead."

Laszlo sighed. "At least the guy was kind enough to wait until we were done questioning Lance."

CHAPTER 15

BACK IN THE vehicle Laszlo drove out of the parking lot and said to Geir, "Now that the cops are here, and the sniper is long gone, what do you suggest is our next avenue?"

"I want to go home," Minx said painfully. "Just take a time-out from all this."

Without a word he took a quick right and then a left. Darkness was already falling. After Lance had been killed, Laszlo called Officer Carson Everett and waited until he'd arrived on the scene. Minx listened as Laszlo shared everything that had happened, but he'd been worried about Minx. Carson had said it was okay to take her away.

Minx had heard all the comments. But she had to admit to being mostly on autopilot. It had been Laszlo directing her back to the vehicle and now it was Laszlo making the decisions.

"Do you want to pick up any food?" Geir asked her.

She shook her head. "I don't want to eat." She started to shiver. "I just want to go home. I want to get into bed. I want to curl up and try to forget how absolutely nightmarish my life has become."

"I'm not sure it will make you feel any better, but I doubt his execution had anything to do with your case."

"How do we know that?"

"We don't, but Carson also promised he would go and

pick up your boss."

"Sure, but he hasn't got him yet, has he? And then he'll probably get bail. He'll get out and torment me and or somebody else in the meantime. You know how this shit works. They create all kinds of chaos while they're loose. There's no guarantee I'm safe even now."

The men stayed silent.

She sagged into the seat. "I'm sorry. I'm just not myself."

"Understandable."

They drove in silence to her place. With relief she saw her own car off to the side. Geir hopped out first, letting her out of the center seat. They walked into her apartment, but Laszlo insisted on going in first, and Geir insisted on her waiting until he'd given the all clear.

She muttered, "See? You don't think it's clear and safe either, do you?"

"It's just a safety precaution," he said gently.

She shrugged, walked inside, took a look around and kept on going to her bedroom. Instead of getting changed for the night, since it was still so early, she threw herself on the bed and pulled the quilt over her. She'd almost shut the door, but it was still open a crack. She didn't bother getting up. Maybe she'd hear what they were talking about. Maybe she didn't care anymore.

She curled up in a ball and thought about everything that had happened. It had been enough of a shock to see how much hate Lance had had for her and to hear what had happened to Mouse after he had left her. She really struggled with the concept of who Mouse had become. These men had said he was a good man. But any man who cheated, lied, paid, or did whatever he could to get into the navy and to become one of the elite SEALs without doing the actual hard work involved wasn't anybody she could respect. And the fact she was thinking that about her best friend from her childhood really hurt.

She remembered how needy she'd been, needing him. How he'd been very loyal to his mother. And maybe that was the only way he could survive. Minx certainly hadn't done any better. But after Poppy had gotten his hands on Mouse, he'd changed in many ways. She hadn't understood, being just a child. And she had kept him on that pedestal all these years. And now she realized he'd fallen from the pedestal. He didn't deserve to be up there in the first place. She had only put him up there based on her own need to have somebody to look up to. And now it was just plain hard to consider who he had become. She wanted to respect the man he was.

These men, both Laszlo and Geir, seemed to have cared a lot about him. And that, at least, was a saving grace. The fact was, her own world was tumbling down around her, but she still had the whole Mouse issue to deal with.

She thought about her asshole of a boss and how he'd made life so difficult for her. And she knew it wasn't just her. But how long before the cops tracked down the other women? How long before the cops took the time to interview the office workers? How long before they picked up Andrew for questioning? How long before they didn't believe his bullshit? She knew now the cops had Laszlo's two tape recordings and the data received off the two hit men's phones and now Lance's all copied on their own servers. She hoped it would be enough to pick up Andrew on the murder-for-hire plot too.

He'd gone from harassment and sexual assault to a murderer. That certainly moved the case up in the ranks of priority for the cops. For that she should be grateful. But, until Andrew was tossed in jail, and his whole career was gone, and everybody else could see and hear what he'd done, she knew she wasn't safe.

Unable to sleep, she pulled herself up against the headboard, grabbed her laptop and checked the calendar. She had a lot of vacation days coming. She didn't know what to do or where to do it, but she would take them. She needed some time off.

She was required by law to give two weeks' notice. She was pretty darn sure she had at least three weeks of vacation days left, but the company would pay her that time out. She had no idea if they'd let her use her vacation as part of her two weeks' notice. Not giving herself a chance to think, she wrote a letter of resignation and attached it to her current supervisor's email.

Just then Laszlo knocked on her door, poked his head around it and asked, "Can we talk?"

She looked up, nodded, looked back down again and hit Send. She closed the laptop, put it off to the side, pulled her knees up to her chest and asked, "What do you want to talk about?"

"I just spoke to Carson."

Her eyebrows lifted. "I didn't hear the phone."

"No, we've turned down the ring tones, in case you were sleeping."

Bitterly she looked around the room. "I tried, but I couldn't sleep."

He sat down on the edge of the bed. "Carson has dispatched some men to pick up your ex-boss. He did say Andrew wasn't at home, and he's not anywhere to be found in his usual haunts. They'll go to the office tomorrow morning and get him."

"If he's there. He obviously had money to pay for my hit. So he could have run too," she said, tiredness pulling at her. "Everybody else will protect him anyway."

"Not once they hear the tapes, see the texts. Not once they realize just what he's done and how bad it's been."

"What else did Carson say?"

"He said he knows your boss's potential father-in-law. And he'll talk to him tonight. I think the wedding is set for ten days later."

She snorted. "Well, ten days of warning is better than being left at the altar or, in this case, better than marrying the asshole." She scrubbed her face. "I'm so tired of all this."

"I know, and you must be careful tonight especially. At least until they pick him up."

She shook her head. "It won't make any difference. If you can't convince the father-in-law-to-be of Andrew's guilt, he'll post bail, and the asshole will be out on the streets again. He tried to kill me once. He'll try again."

"We know that, and that's why we're staying here tonight, and we'll be on watch for the full twenty-four hours. Geir will be upstairs. I'll be here with you, and then we'll switch out."

She nodded slowly. "Did I ever say *thank you*? Because I really do appreciate that you stayed to help look after me. I'd be dead a couple times over by now, I'm sure."

"It's been a pretty rough go. But we are here," he said firmly. "And life will improve once we get past this."

"What are you going to do?"

"Tomorrow or the next day? Head back home to New Mexico. Then we'll see. We need to go to California and get to the bottom of this Mouse stuff."

"I wish I could come with you. But it's not to be. At

least not at the moment."

"It would be more dangerous than ever to involve you in our mess," he admitted. "You need to stay here and get your life together."

She gave him a wry look. "Well, I already made a decision and took action that will change my life in a big way."

"What did you do?" he asked, suddenly straightening on the bed.

"I handed in my resignation. As of two weeks from now, I'm done," she said firmly.

He stared at her in surprise, then laughed. "When you make a change, you make a big one."

She shrugged. "Only a big change will get me out of this hell."

"But at least you've done it. Now what you need to do is figure out in the next two weeks where you want to go. Make that decision and follow through."

She nodded. "I know. More big decisions. But just having handed in my resignation, I do feel a lot better. I've met a bunch of people over the years. I might contact some of them and look for job possibilities."

"Do you want to return to your uncle's in Maine?"

She shook her head. "No, I kind of feel like I'm done with that. I want to move on somewhere new, somewhere different. I was thinking California, but, after hearing about Poppy and Mouse going there, that's the last place I want to be."

"California's a huge state," he said with a big grin. "And there's an awful lot more to it than just Coronado."

She nodded. "But there's a taint to it now for me."

"Understood."

Just then Geir called from the living room.

Laszlo reached over, gently squeezing her hand. "I'll be right back." He got up and walked out to the living room. "What's up, Geir?"

She just barely heard the excitement in his voice as he said, "Heard from Levi. He and Mason both want to talk with us."

"About Mouse?"

"Yeah. Both of them remember."

She bounded off her bed and raced out to the living room. "That's a talk I want to be involved in. Mouse was my friend too."

The two men looked at her, then at each other and nodded.

Minx asked, "When will you talk to them?"

"In the morning. We're setting up a conference call."

She nodded. "For me, nine a.m. is good. I'm not going to work anyway." She turned and headed back to her room; then she stopped and said, "It's been hours since you guys ate. Do you need food?"

Geir smiled. "I'll slip around the corner. I think I saw Chinese takeout. I'll pick up enough food for all of us."

She smiled. "That would be nice. In that case, do you mind if I go lie down again?"

Both men shook their heads.

Geir said, "I'll be at least a few minutes anyway. I want to do a search around the neighborhood to make sure we don't have anybody coming in who we aren't expecting."

She turned and looked worriedly at Laszlo. "Are you staying close?"

He nodded.

Geir got up, grabbed Laszlo's keys and said with a backward glance, "I'll be back in an hour with food." And he walked out.

She smiled at Laszlo. "Definitely going to lie down. I'm really cold."

"I'll put on the teakettle and bring you a cup of tea. It might be better if you don't sleep at this hour. You still need to get a decent night's rest later this evening."

She smiled and nodded. "That's a theory. But thinking about all the things that have happened makes sleep hard to come by. Who knew meeting you—was it just yesterday?— would blow my world so far apart that it can't be put back together again."

"It can be. It can, just in a different way, a better way," he promised.

She gave him a shuttered look. "But can it? I don't have the group of friends you have. I don't have that community. I felt terribly alone growing up. Mouse made my life so much easier. But I have to admit, coming back here, I've gotten a whole new perspective on Mouse too. And it's not terribly pleasant."

"Remember your childhood memories. And keep them happy, keep them contained. Don't let all this taint that."

"Too late," she tossed over her shoulder. She could hear him in the kitchen putting the teakettle on.

A few minutes later he came to her open bedroom door. "Do you want anything in your tea?"

She shook her head. "I'll just have a cup black, please."

In her mind she wondered if she could do something to make this not quite so traumatizing. And she also had to figure out where to move to. Especially now that she no longer had a job. She had money in the bank, not tons, but she didn't spend any, just paid her bills. And then there was the matter of what she was planning to do with the rest of her life.

"Pretty sad smile on your face," Laszlo said gently as he walked in with her tea. "What are you thinking about?"

"About how everything I've done so far in life sucks, and now I'm looking at the rest of my life, wondering what to do."

He gave a chuckle. "Yep, been there myself. Two years ago, the accident was a major turning point."

She smiled and nodded. "I feel like I'm at another one."

"You are," he said gently. "But that doesn't mean it has to be difficult or wrong."

She snuggled deeper in the covers. "When you two leave, I'll really be alone. How come I feel closer to you two than I've felt to anybody in a long time? It's pretty unnerving."

"We slipped in under your guard, touched a nerve, ripped a couple scabs off old wounds, made you take a good look at life." His tone was serious. "And when you do things like that, you get to know people on a very deep level very quickly."

"And what if I don't want to lose contact?" She gave him a challenging stare. What she really wanted was for him to hold her and to tell her that it would all be okay. Yet that acknowledged a little girl was still inside her, looking for somebody else to fix her life, to fix all that was wrong. And she knew better. But, for just that one moment, she wished she could be that little girl again.

"You don't have to. I fully expected to update you when we find out what happened with Mouse."

"Do you really think it's not the same man?"

He walked around the bed and sat at the headboard beside her. "I think we must keep an open mind. A part of me wants to believe there were two of them. So that the Mouse I knew hadn't gone through all this shit. But I can't be sure of that. His body was badly scarred. He resembles the photo you have of him as a kid. Maybe the conference call in the morning will bring us some answers. But I don't know for sure."

She nodded and curled deeper into the blankets. "Do you mind if I just nod off for a little bit? I'm so cold."

He shifted and moved her gently closer against him. "Go ahead and sleep. When the Chinese food comes, I'll wake you up."

She smiled, let her head drop on his chest and eased into a restful sleep.

LASZLO GENTLY STROKED her back, his mind whirling with all the information they'd come up with. In fact, it had been a lot of information very quickly, and his mind still hadn't really adapted or absorbed any of it. To think of all the things that he'd known about Mouse, it was pretty painful to hear the newest information. And yet how much of it was true and how much of it was an angry, spiteful outburst from a man who'd felt rejected by Mouse? And what the hell was going on with Mouse and this Poppy guy?

To think somebody could have cheated their way into the US Naval Academy was just something Laszlo couldn't understand. Granted, Laszlo could see how an ace computer hacker could replace one guy's face with another guy's, even in a government database. But you still had to go through all the physical exercises. So how had all that happened? The only way for it to work was if this new SEAL was coming in from another part of the country. Likely back East. But still, files had to be created, histories created, backgrounds, tests, all that stuff had to be forged. And yet what Laszlo did know was it didn't seem to matter exactly what anyone did. Money always got you what you wanted. Even in the navy it seemed. As long as it was something tangible that could be purchased.

But Mouse would have had to overcome his fear of the water regardless.

Their unit had teased him and bugged him terribly but never about swimming, as far as Laszlo could remember. But then they had teased him about his days on leave all the time too. He'd been well-known for heading to third-world countries, and the guys had wondered at the time, why? What was the draw? But Mouse never really said. They figured it was just because it was cheap booze, easy sex. But there were no easy answers. The fact that there were so many unanswered questions no longer bothered Laszlo because he knew it was all about to break apart. As in *wide apart.*

The meeting in the morning should help a lot too. He needed his laptop to go over some of the information they got from Lance's phone today and also the conversations with Carson. Laszlo needed to make sure Minx was no longer in danger from her ex-boss before Laszlo and Geir left for Santa Fe and beyond to California.

Laszlo loved it that she'd quit. Sometimes when life handed you lemons, the best thing you could do was make lemon cheesecake out of it. And, in this case, maybe it would be the best option for her. It was obvious she wasn't happy, and she deserved to be. She'd had as shitty a life as Mouse had. Although she'd taken a better exit road than he had.

And how did Laszlo feel about her wanting to stay in touch? He grinned. He'd been trying to figure out how to suggest it himself. She was dynamite. And he had to admit, he had a lot of respect for somebody who had been where she was and how she'd handled herself even today. He figured they were probably a long way away from anything more than that, but it was hard to say.

Just then she twisted and whimpered beside him. He gently stroked her arms and back.

But she cried out, "No, no, don't touch. Hands off. Get away from me." Her arms flailed about. Suddenly she bawled like a little child.

His heart broke as he realized just how ugly her life must have been. He would wait to get his laptop; he couldn't leave her like that. He tucked her into his arms until she lay across his chest, and he just held her. Over and over again he whispered, "It's okay. You're fine. It's okay. You'll be fine. Let it go. Just sleep."

And finally she did. She took a deep breath and relaxed against his chest, her hand stroking his cheek and his lips, and she whispered, "Laszlo?"

He couldn't help himself. He dropped a kiss on her temple and whispered, "Yes. You were crying out in pain, as if caught up in a nightmare. I couldn't let you suffer like that."

She shifted her head back, and her sleepy gaze stared up at him. There was such a sweet innocence there, and yet he knew how worldly her upbringing had been. "You look adorable."

"Ha." She didn't try to move away. Instead she dropped her head back down again, wrapped her arms around him and said, "Thank you."

"For what?" he asked, gently massaging her back.

"For sticking around. For holding me. For caring enough to make sure the nightmares didn't grab me again."

"Again?"

"Yes, a couple times I had to fight off being raped," she whispered. "Even now, when I get super tired or super worried, the memories grab ahold and don't let go."

He could feel the rage catching the back of his throat.

She smiled. "It was a long time ago."

"But you don't forget, do you?" he asked with certainty.

"No. But then you don't forget your accident either, do you?"

He shook his head. "No, I don't."

She rolled over, half-sitting, propped her arms on his chest and looked up at him. "We're both the walking wounded. One of us physically and the other emotionally."

He smiled. "You're still very beautiful to me. I'm the opposite."

She shook her head. "I don't know about the beautiful part. That's always made me very wary."

He could understand.

"Beautiful children were always attacked first."

"Well, you're safe with me."

She grinned, a twinkle coming into her eye. "And how safe is that? And what if I don't want to be safe with you?"

And he froze, caught by her gaze and the heat she had absolutely no trouble letting him see. He stared down at her, his finger stroking her cheek. "Are you trying to seduce me?" he asked in fascination, heat unfurling deep inside his gut. "Because if you are …" He leaned forward, his lips hovering tantalizingly close to hers. "Then I'm definitely interested."

She slid a hand up his chest, around his neck, making his toes curl in delight. Then she reached long fingers into his scalp and tugged him closer. "Then what's stopping you?"

He closed the distance and kissed her.

CHAPTER 16

S HE KNEW IT'D be like that with him. There was just no way it wouldn't be. He was such a strong alpha male, it was seriously impossible to miss just how much passion and control, how much power he exuded. And she wanted to taste that. She wanted to know what it felt like to touch fire—controlled fire—and not be hurt. She kissed him with longing. Her arms wrapped tight around his neck. Holding him close. His arms crushed her ribs so she was flattened against him, her breasts plastered against his chest.

And she suddenly realized just how much she missed this. How alone she had been all these years. She'd had several relationships, but she hadn't let herself care. Not really. She'd remember the loss and the betrayal of those she had cared for. And how quickly she'd learned they wouldn't be here for her over the long haul. Relationships had become fast, simple, easy.

It wasn't what she wanted this time. She'd heard him talk about his relationships with his buddies, and she'd missed that stage of life. She never had sleepovers with girlfriends. She never had shopping in the mall, getting her nails done, giggling and laughing about graduation. She'd graduated but hadn't attended the ceremony. She'd never gone to a party; she hadn't been tempted by any of that. None of it mattered. All she wanted was tonight with him.

His kiss deepened, his tongue sliding between her lips, dueling with hers.

A groan whispered through his chest to hang between them, before his lips closed once again over hers. He twisted her in his arms so she lay flat on the bed, and he rose over her. His kisses were hard, punishing, as if he wanted to do more but couldn't start anything.

And then she realized it was something else. She opened her eyes. "What?"

He hesitated, then whispered, "Geir is coming back soon."

She narrowed her gaze at him. "That would not be good."

He kissed her hard again, whispering, "I know."

Just then they heard the door, and he bowed his head, his eyes closed, and whispered, "I don't suppose we could pick this up later?"

She grabbed his ears, pulled him up so she could stare into his eyes and whispered, "You better. As soon as he goes out to do whatever he's doing on watch, you have an appointment here. Don't be late."

He chuckled and rolled off. Standing, he rearranged his jeans.

She smiled as she saw the size of the bulge in his pants. She gently stroked the material, hearing his gasp, seeing the shudder and the red roll through his cheeks as he threw his head back. And she whispered, "Hold that thought."

"You're a tease," he ground out.

She hopped off the bed, walked toward the bathroom. "Nope, no teasing allowed. Only promises."

In the bathroom she washed her face, brushed her teeth, and, when she was done, she studied her face in the mirror and smiled. If nothing else, their interrupted foreplay had put a sparkle in her cheeks. The gaze that looked back at her had a luminescence she hadn't seen before. She wanted tonight. She wanted it really badly. If any asshole came between her and Laszlo, she swore she'd take him out all on her own.

When she walked out to the kitchen, Geir was sitting down with a large bag of takeout food in front of him. "I don't know if you want plates or to just eat out of the containers, but I bought lots."

She sat down, reached for a fork that somebody had already collected and said, "Good, because I'm famished."

Geir looked up, and she caught the twinkle in his gaze. She shook her head. "Not a word."

He pinched his lips together in a mock show of being obedient and then chuckled.

Dinner was dispatched very quickly. The talk turned to wondering about various theories but with no complete answers coming. They were in a stage of waiting. With Carson, with Levi, with Mason, all these men were working on her case and on Mouse's case, and still ... she didn't know anything yet.

At least the conversation was good, supportive. Lots of laughter, lots of friendliness. And through it all she didn't dare look directly at Laszlo because she knew what she'd see. She felt bad for Geir. It was obvious he had interrupted them and planned to tease them.

Finally Geir finished his food, sat back and said, "Now, shall I go pick up coffee or do you want to put on a pot?"

She stood. "We didn't stop and get any coffee to make a pot."

"No. I'll add it to my list." Geir got up, collected all the garbage and said, "I'll take this out. You might as well put the leftovers in the fridge for later. He'll probably need it." His tone was dry. "And I'll head out. I won't grab to-go coffee for you guys obviously, but I'll pick myself up one, and then a pound for tomorrow and do a full sweep outside."

That started a conversation as to what the rest of their plan was.

"I thought you would be upstairs," Minx said.

"I will be once I've checked the area." He gave them a brief smile, then said over his shoulder at the front door, "Enjoy yourselves." And he left.

As soon as the door shut, she broke out in laughter. "Oh, my God, that was too priceless."

Laszlo turned to her. "How much of this did you find funny?" He looked at her in mock anger.

She wrapped her arms around his neck and said, "He's gone."

Instantly Laszlo's arms crushed her against him. "Now can we pick up where we left off? It's a little earlier than you said."

"That's okay. We can get in some extra practice."

He chuckled, and, with his arms wrapped around her, he had her walking backward, their bodies pinned from hip to chest. "Maybe you need it, sweetie, but I shouldn't."

At that she grinned. "Oh, this is a male thing, isn't it?"

He shook his head. "No, it's not a male thing. It's just a you-and-me thing."

And before she realized it, she was flat on the bed, and he ravaged her like she'd never been ravaged before. She couldn't get enough. Her hands stroked his body, pulling his shirt out from his jeans. She really wanted where that fascinating bulge was hidden, but he wouldn't let her get that close. Every time she tried, he kissed her senseless, until she just lay there gasping, trying to figure out where her center of balance had gone. And, as soon as she did that, he trailed kisses down her until he had her shirt off and was suckling her nipple through her soft cotton bra. She arched her back off the bed, twisting and turning, welcoming his attention, loving the distraction, yet desperately in need of so much more.

"It's not fair. If my clothes are coming off, I want to see you too."

"But you're beautiful. I'm just battered and worn."

"You're beautiful too," she said softly. "And every one of those scars is a reminder of what you've survived."

But he took her lips in another drugging kiss until she couldn't do anything but sag against him.

"Oh, my God, you kiss so beautifully," she murmured, her body pliant, soft. "I could stay here and kiss you all day."

At that, he slid fingers inside her jeans, just to the edge of the soft folds of her skin, and stroked her one stroke, which had her screaming.

"Oh, my God. I was lying." She quickly shifted out of his range, removed her bra, skidded out of her jeans, tossed her panties with them, and then, still wearing brown cotton socks, lay on the bed spread-eagled. She reached up, her arms going around his neck.

He shook his head. "You're still wearing too much. He lifted one leg, gently stroking his hand down the top of her thigh, under her calf, to her foot and pulled off her sock. But before he was done, he kissed the arch of her foot.

She shrieked with laughter. "That tickles."

But he wouldn't let her escape. With his tongue, he

lapped up the side of her foot and around her ankle. He continued to drop kisses along her leg, and, at the back of her knee, he stopped, giving it particular attention.

She twisted, half torn by the tickling, half caught by the erotic emotions. She wanted to touch him. She wanted to taste him. And he wasn't letting her. As soon as she got her foot out of his grasp, he turned his attention to the other one. By the time he was up to her knee, she was moaning, her hips writhing in front of him.

He placed one hand on either side of her hips and held her down; then he lowered his head and tasted. She screamed, her hips rising up to meet him, and he feasted on the bounty before him.

She was mindless with joy, her body screaming for more, and finally she grasped his hair in her hands and pulled him up to make sure he listened to her.

He chuckled as he slid his tongue past her belly button, between her breasts, under her neck and her chin, before latching onto her lips, kissing her again and again.

She slid her hands inside his jeans, cupping the erection she was desperate to touch.

He gave a guttural groan, slipped out of her reach and quickly stripped down. When he stood before her, he didn't give her a chance to look at him. He threw himself on top of her, shifted the angle she lay in and, with his erection poised at the center of her, plunged in deep.

She cried out, and he froze. She shook her head. "More. More."

And he set that into motion, with her chanting for more, always more. He plunged harder, deeper, faster, taking them both to a crescendo, then pushing them over.

By the time he collapsed on top of her, she was barely

breathing. She was still gasping for breath, waiting for her heart to slow down, her body boneless, her mind empty.

He groaned and slowly rolled to the side. Held his weight on his arm. "Okay, now I'm dead," he muttered softly.

"That makes two of us," she whispered.

He wrapped an arm around her and pulled her up close.

"Even that motion is too much for me," she whispered. "I don't think I could move on my own."

"You don't need to. We are just going to lie here until we feel better."

She chuckled. "I couldn't feel any better."

He stroked the hair off her forehead and dropped a kiss on her temple. "Good." His voice said he was satisfied. "That's the way it should be."

She wrapped her arms around him. "You know? We could have done this before he came in with the food."

He chuckled. "We could have, if you woke up sooner. I don't know about you, but I wasn't planning on getting dressed right away or anytime soon or going out and meeting people."

"Good point." She let her hand stroke his chest. Her fingers eased from one scar to the next. And there were some big ones. "Lost a few organs, didn't you?"

"Yeah, I did. Muscles and skin too. There were surgeries to replace skin, surgeries to reattach muscles, surgeries to put in bone plates and pins, surgeries to remove a spleen we had hoped would survive but didn't. There too many surgeries."

She stroked her hand down the top of his thighs and over his knee. "You *are* beautiful, you know that?" She rose up onto her knees and studied him.

"How can you say this broken body is beautiful?" he protested.

She placed a finger against his lips. "Because it's a warrior's body. You asked it to do something superhuman, and it responded in kind. It rebuilt itself when it had no business doing that. It survived when anybody else would have given up the ghost and died. Not only survived, look at you. You're positively thriving. You're walking and talking. You're powerful." She shook her head. "And that is something I respect. You didn't give up."

"I wanted to," he said, his voice dark. "Many times."

She nodded. "Of course you did. Anybody would have in that situation."

He shrugged. "I don't know about that, but I know, in the dark of the night, I didn't think I'd make it. I didn't know that I wanted to make it."

She smiled, straddled his body, her fingers stroking, exploring the multiple indents, scar tissue, hills of his body, a body unlike any other male she'd ever known. He was right. He was battered. But it wasn't scars of shame. They were scars of honor.

"And how about now?" She settled on top of his thighs. She leaned down and kissed each scar as she came to it, taking the time to admire how well it had healed, how his body had responded by accepting the wound and making it part of him.

He gently stroked her back. "I might need a little bit of time before we go at it again."

"Really?" She slid a hand down his ribs, across his belly, sliding it into the curls below and chuckled.

He groaned. "Okay, scratch that."

Her hand closed around him, feeling him lurch against

her fingers, wanting everything she had to give. And she had a lot. Her life seemed so alone, so empty. And as he filled her, she was more than grateful to give him what he needed.

LASZLO COULDN'T BELIEVE he was quite where he was. But he was overjoyed. Not only had she not been turned off by his broken body, it hadn't seemed to faze her. If anything, she'd been thrilled by everything she saw. He had to wonder at that. But then he was biased. He'd known what he was before. He'd always been proud of his physique, his fitness level, his strength. There was nothing like having all that knocked out in an accident, erased in just one instant, and his whole world changed to make him appreciate what he had now versus what he had then. Because what he had now, he'd worked so hard to get. Before it had been a gift, a gift of genetics, part of his training, something he had rejoiced in. But what he had now, he'd worked every damn day to get to.

He knew how much pain he'd been in, how much sweat he'd worked up, how much effort it had taken to get here. And he didn't take it lightly anymore. He appreciated every damn muscle that worked because, for a long time, so many hadn't. With her sleeping in his arms, he kept stroking, hugging her. He couldn't get enough. He didn't want the night to end. He didn't want to leave, not if it meant leaving her behind. She'd handed in her resignation. He knew it was damn fast, but it was no faster than Honey and Erick, or Faith and Cade. And now there was Talon and Clary.

Although Talon and Clary had known each other years earlier. Regardless Laszlo wanted what they all had, what Badger and Kat had. Hell, what Levi and Ice had. What

Mason and Tesla had. What a lot of their teams had going on too. Laszlo had hoped to find what they had. He just hadn't expected to. And now that he had it, a part of him was worried it wasn't as strong, it wasn't as good, it wasn't as real. But it didn't take long, lying in the dark as he was, to realize that was fear talking. He was scared to lose what he had and scared what he'd found would disappear with the light of day. Maybe he was just a one-night stand to her. He hoped not because he wanted so much more.

"What are you thinking?" she asked sleepily.

He stroked her hair off her forehead. "You should be sleeping."

"You're thinking too loud." She smiled.

That surprised a laugh out of him. "I was thinking I don't want to lose contact with you."

"Good. I already told you that I wanted to stay in touch."

"Come to New Mexico. Even just for a couple days. See how you like it. You can go anywhere in the world. There's no reason to come to New Mexico over any other place, except this," he said.

She raised her head and looked at him. "This? As in sex?"

He chuckled. "The sex is magnificent," he said with a teasing smile. "But I meant *us*." He frowned. "I'm not very good at this kind of stuff."

Her gaze gentled as she stared at him. "You're doing fine."

He shook his head. "No, I'm not because I don't know how to express how full I feel, how happy I am inside. How much I admire who you are, what you've survived. And how much I don't want to let go of that. I want to figure out what we have, if this is the start of something fantastic or if it's just for tonight."

She stretched her fingers, sliding across the bottom part of his leg and said, "I was never into one-night stands. And I have to tell you that I never *ever* allowed myself to feel for somebody again because I knew that to open myself up was to end in pain. And I was done with pain. I was done with loss. I was done with abandonment. But, in your case, I've already opened up my heart further, deeper and wider than I ever have before. So I'd better go to New Mexico. Because otherwise you'd be abandoning me."

"Well, I can't do that," he said softly. "That would be extremely dishonorable of me."

She smiled and whispered, "And what you are is a man of honor."

He grinned. "Always."

Just then they heard a sound outside her bedroom window. Instantly he shifted and slid out from under her. He quickly pulled on his boxers and jeans, tossed his T-shirt over his head and held his finger against her lips. "Stay quiet."

She handed him his phone.

He wasn't sure where the hell he'd lost it. He quickly texted Geir with **Noises outside.**

The response was immediate. **Yes, rear of the house. Watch your back.**

Laszlo slipped into the kitchen and, without turning on the lights, checked out the window to see if anyone was there. Being a basement apartment, they were at ground level. He watched the front of the house but couldn't see anything. Slipping to the living room, he checked there. He thought he saw a shadow outside, coming around the corner.

He sent Geir another text, letting him know. Pocketing his cell phone, he stepped behind the main door, watching as Minx, fully dressed, came out of the bedroom.

He held up a hand to stop her, motioned her back toward the bedroom. She disappeared. He waited. Sure enough, the doorknob turned. As the front door pushed open, Laszlo realized that either Geir hadn't locked it as he went out—not possible—or this asshole had a key. How hard would it be to have gotten a copy of her key? If he worked in the same office as Minx, probably not hard at all.

The door opened with a slight squeak. The person on the other side froze, and, when he couldn't hear anything, he pushed it open just that much more. Laszlo waited until the man was fully in the room. Just as he was about to jump on the intruder, he caught sight of the handgun in the man's hand. Laszlo came up behind him and caught him in a headlock, tripped him and dropped him to the floor. But whoever this guy was, he was big, strong and fast. He was also mean as a snake.

He dropped, turned, reached up with his legs, kicked, spun around with his right hand fisted and caught Laszlo in the jaw. But Laszlo was already moving out of the way and took a slight clip, not the full force of his blow. Ignoring the screaming pain in his back, he twisted, turned, slammed his hand down on the man's wrist, his fingers releasing the gun, and Laszlo kicked it, making it skitter across the room. The man threw an arm around Laszlo's neck, trying to choke him as he went down and rolled on top of him.

That crocodile move was a death grip, but Laszlo hadn't been through heavy military training for nothing. He rose up on his knees, trying not to wince at the pain, slammed an elbow into the man's lower abdomen, reached up and around, and pressed a finger into his eyeball. The man roared. Laszlo moved quickly, flipping the intruder, and was once again on top. He reached around the man's neck, grabbed his chin and pulled back to the point he could snap his neck. Of the gun there was no sign.

"Enough," Laszlo roared.

But the man wasn't listening. "Fuck you," he roared. "The stupid bitch. Figures she'd have some asshole here to fuck her. Apparently she's completely useless without a man."

In the silence that followed, the *click* of a gun hammer being pulled back was heard.

"What did you just say about me?" Minx asked, her voice hard and cold. Lights flicked on, and she glared down at the man in front of her. "Well, well, well. Look at that. Since when were house calls part of your job?"

"Is it him?" Laszlo asked.

She nodded. "It so is."

Just then Geir came sliding in through the front door, took one look, and, in a move Geir had perfected a long time ago, hit a pressure point between the man's neck and shoulder, and he dropped cold on the floor. "I'm not sure he's alone," he said to Laszlo.

Minx motioned to Laszlo. "Head down the hall. I'll stand watch over him." She still had the gun in her hand.

He glanced at her. "Do you know how to use that?"

She gave him a hard glance. "Since I was about six," she said mockingly.

He took a close look at her face, realized she was really okay and then raced down the hall.

He slid into the back room where the door to the upstairs was. And found it open. He shook his head and swiftly moved to the bottom of the stairs. There were no lights on upstairs either. He peered upward but couldn't see or hear anything. As soon as he stepped on those stairs, he knew there would be creaks. Every old house creaked. He grabbed the two handrails and, using them, leveraged himself up to land gently six steps up. And then did it again. He didn't know if it was any more silent, but it was certainly unorthodox, and not what anybody would be expecting.

Just as he was about to turn a corner at the top landing, where there was a short wall, he thought he heard a sound nearby, a grunt and a half cry as if somebody had landed wrong as he came down. And then there were running feet. And in a second unusual move, he jumped over the railing, over the short wall, landing in the upper hallway.

Laszlo gave chase, hitting the hallway light switch as the man bolted for the upstairs kitchen. And just as he raced through the kitchen, Geir came through the rear kitchen door, and the intruder ran right into Geir's right hook.

Laszlo hit another light switch to see the second intruder sprawled on the upstairs kitchen floor. He looked over at Geir's right hand and said, "You should patent that sucker."

Geir grinned. "It is pretty deadly."

Between the two of them, they got the intruder up and on Laszlo's shoulder, and he carefully made his way down the stairs, dropping the second man on the floor beside the first one. Still heaving and trying to catch his breath, Laszlo pulled out his phone and called Carson.

"What the hell is the matter with you?" Carson snapped. "Don't you ever sleep?"

"We had been sleeping just fine until somebody tried to come in and kill Minx. And he brought a buddy again."

"New hit men?" Carson asked, his voice rising in shock.

"No. He decided to make the trip himself."

With excitement brimming in his voice, Carson said, "Please, please, *please* tell me it's him."

"Oh, it's him. He came in with a gun. Somehow he also had a key to her apartment. And then the second man came in through the upstairs, ready to come down the stairs and take her out or give Conley a hand if he ran into trouble."

"I'll be there in fifteen minutes," the officer said, almost singing. And he hung up.

Laszlo turned to find Geir wrapping ties around the men's arms and legs. "Carson is on his way."

As soon as the men were secured, Minx held out the gun to Laszlo. "I might know how to use them, but I hate them."

He took the weapon from her hand and checked it. "Not only is it loaded, there's one in the chamber."

He placed it on the counter out of everybody's reach, then pulled her into his arms. She wrapped her arms tight around him, hugging him hard. He waited until she calmed down and just nestled in closer.

She turned slightly, looking into the room in general. "Is it over finally?"

"You know? I think it probably is," Geir said. "He brought his own backup this time. We caught the handler, who somebody assassinated, and we took out of play the first two hit men. Now we got the man himself responsible for it all and his partner. So I'd say it's pretty well a clean sweep."

She smiled brilliantly. "I'm so damn glad."

"So," Geir said, "are you coming back with us, or is Laszlo staying with you?"

She looked at him in confusion. But at the rumbling chuckle coming from Laszlo's chest, her surprise turned to suspicion. "What are you talking about?"

Geir studied her with a mocking look and said, "Well, you're only renting this place for a month at a time. You've handed in your resignation. And you're looking for a place to move. I figured, since you and Laszlo hooked up, you'd be moving into his place."

She flushed, shaking her head. "I'll go visit for a few days. See how it goes," she said cautiously. "I'm not one to jump into things."

Geir stared at her, but the corner of his lips twitched. "So, jumping into bed with Laszlo tonight wasn't jumping into anything?"

She fisted her hands on her hips and glared at him. "Are you being cheeky?"

He raised his eyebrows, shaking his head. "No, ma'am." He turned, walking over to the coffeepot. "Damn, I left the coffee in the truck." He tossed Laszlo a quick glance. "I'll be right back."

As the door shut behind him, she turned to Laszlo. "Does he really think I'll move in with you? Just after that?"

He smiled. "It's happened to several of our friends. I think he figured I was the next one to get lucky."

"*Lucky?*" she said in an ominous tone. "What kind of *lucky?*"

"The kind of lucky that I'm hoping to get over and over and over again," he said. "But more than that, the lucky that says you care about me and I care about you, and we're more than happy to take steps with arms around each other toward whatever the future brings."

She could feel tears welling in her eyes, dripping from the corners down her cheek. "Now *that* kind of lucky," she whispered, "I can get behind."

CHAPTER 17

B Y THE TIME Officer Everett arrived, the coffeepot had once again been filled and emptied and was now dripping again. The man was positively dancing. Both of the intruders were now awake.

Andrew glared at Minx and said, "You know you're fired."

She laughed outright. "I already resigned."

He stared at her. "So why are you giving me all this trouble?"

"Because you're an asshole," she snapped. "And I don't want you doing that to any more women."

"They liked it," he said. "What can I say? Women fall all over me."

She shook her head. "You don't get it, do you?"

He just glared at her and shut up.

She looked down at his buddy. "Really? You hung your shingle up with this guy? Haven't you figured out he's a loser?"

"He promised me a lot of money," said the much younger man with long hair.

"And what's a lot of money to you?"

He stared at her resentfully. "I'm supposed to get a grand if the night went off without a hitch."

She leaned forward and in a confidential voice said,

"Next time get the cash up front." And she backed off, watching as the two men were hauled out to the police cruiser.

"Make sure you come in for a statement in the morning," Carson said. "I want to get this wrapped up tight as a barrel before noon."

"Do you need forensic evidence?"

"We'll get the guys in here and run fingerprints and check the doorknobs, etc. But just to make sure we have the forensic evidence to go along with the witnesses' statements."

She smiled and nodded. "No problem. I'll come in before we leave town."

The officer stopped and looked at her. "You're leaving?"

"Laszlo and I are traveling back to New Mexico in my car."

Beside her, she heard Geir shout with laughter. "Geir will drive alone because he's insufferable." She beamed. "However, if you need me to come back for the trial, that is absolutely no problem. I'm sure these two will be happy to return with me and to make sure this asshole goes away for a long time."

Carson nodded. "We might need you too. It's hard to say at this point as Angela Davis and Melinda Barry have both stepped forward now. We'll get the details from you in the morning then. Make sure you don't leave town without coming by and seeing me."

"Not a problem," she swore.

As soon as they were gone, she turned, looked at the two men, spun around and danced into the kitchen. "It's over. Over." She raced to Geir, threw her arms around him and gave him a great big hug.

He hugged her back. "Welcome to the family."

She stepped back with misty eyes. "Thank you. That's the nicest thing anybody has said to me in my life." She walked over to find Laszlo, his arms already open and waiting for her. She snuggled in tight. "Now can we get some sleep finally? I'm really tired."

He squeezed her and then slung one arm around her shoulders. "Come on, sweetie. Back to bed with you."

"Now that's the best suggestion I've heard in a long time."

"Me too." And he squeezed her tight again, as if he'd never let her go.

Thank heavens.

EPILOGUE

G EIR PAVLA WATCHED the pair head back to Minx's bedroom. He was happy for his friend. Laszlo had been through so much shit and so much hurt. Minx didn't even know about his father in Norway, Geir was pretty sure. There hadn't been time. But apparently that was how life was these days. He'd watched so many of his friends come together in a combustible mode, work out their differences and, all of a sudden, be a perfect fit. He didn't expect perfection in their lives from their start. It would take time to adapt and to find a way to get along the best they could. But he knew Laszlo and Minx would make it. They were so good for each other. And Geir had no intention of interrupting their initial time together as a couple. As soon as they hit New Mexico, Geir would head to California.

He had a lot of contacts there he wasn't sure the others had. They also had a meeting in the morning. Someone in the group needed to connect with Coronado. He hoped to follow that up with a personal visit to Mason and see if they could get to the bottom of what the hell had happened with Mouse. But Geir hadn't contacted Mason to see if that could happen. At this point, Geir didn't know that he trusted anything he'd heard. None of it made any sense. But he needed to give them all an update too.

He sent out a message to Mason, telling him what happened. Even with another four hours until daylight here in Texas—meaning another six in California—Mason sent back a quick message. **Let's do the meeting when you return to New Mexico then.**

Geir agreed with that decision. The sooner they could get home, the better. He texted Mason again. **After this I'm coming down to Coronado. We're so damn close. And yet we're so far away.**

No, with every clue, you're closer, Mason texted back. **Things are happening right now, so stand strong. We'll get to the bottom of this, and it'll happen fast.**

Sure, but I need a place to stay in Coronado. I may have to call some friends.

I know somebody who runs a B&B. If you want, I can call her and get you a room. Nobody will know who you are, so you don't have to feel beholden to anyone, and you don't have to feel like you need to entertain or be entertained.

Perfect. What's her name?

Her first name is Morning. Morning Blossom.

Geir stared at the name and shook his head. **Really?**

The text came back right away. **Yeah, really. But she's a sweetheart. You'll love her.**

Geir wasn't sure. But how hard could it be to love anybody named Morning Blossom? He grinned, pocketed his phone and headed for Minx's couch. While he had the chance, he would catch a few hours of sleep because, as far as he could see, this was all coming to a head faster than ever. And he doubted he'd get Laszlo to go with him to California. But maybe. If not, well, it was time for Jager to come in out of the dark.

As he lay in the dark, Geir thought about the man he'd called best friend for so long. But Jager had taken the incident the worst. He'd been the navigator in the truck and had blamed himself. And yet, no way in hell was he responsible.

Geir sent Jager a quick message. **I know you're seeing these. I'm heading to Coronado in a couple days. Things have blown open. Road trip?**

He waited and waited, and, when he thought, *No way in hell would Jager break his silence*, Geir got a message. He read it and grinned.

I'll be there.

This concludes Book 5 of SEALs of Steel: Laszlo.

Read about Geir: SEALs of Steel, Book 6

SEALS OF STEEL: GEIR
BOOK 6

When an eight-man unit hit a landmine, all were injured but one died. The remaining seven aim to see Mouse's death avenged.

The more Geir discovers, the more he fears the newest member of his former SEALs team wasn't who they thought.

An artist, Morning runs a B&B. She's avoided relationships but quickly decides she wouldn't mind having Geir around permanently. His protectiveness becomes much more when the nastiness of his world spills into hers...

Book 6 is available now!

To find out more visit Dale Mayer's website.

http://smarturl.it/dmgeir

Author's Note

Thank you for reading Laszlo: SEALs of Steel, Book 5! If you enjoyed the book, please take a moment and leave a short review.

Dear reader,

I love to hear from readers, and you can contact me at my website: www.dalemayer.com or at my Facebook author page. To be informed of new releases and special offers, sign up for my newsletter or follow me on BookBub. And if you are interested in joining Dale Mayer's Fan Club, here is the Facebook sign up page.
facebook.com/groups/402384989872660

Cheers,
Dale Mayer

Your Free Book Awaits!

KILL OR BE KILLED

Part of an elite SEAL team, Mason takes on the dangerous jobs no one else wants to do – or can do. When he's on a mission, he's focused and dedicated. When he's not, he plays as hard as he fights.

Until he meets a woman he can't have but can't forget. Software developer, Tesla lost her brother in combat and has no intention of getting close to someone else in the military. Determined to save other US soldiers from a similar fate, she's created a program that could save lives. But other countries know about the program, and they won't stop until they get it – and get her.

Time is running out ... For her ... For him ... For them ...

DOWNLOAD a *__complimentary__* copy of MASON? Just tell me where to send it!

http://dalemayer.com/sealsmason/

About the Author

Dale Mayer is a USA Today bestselling author best known for her Psychic Visions and Family Blood Ties series. Her contemporary romances are raw and full of passion and emotion (Second Chances, SKIN), her thrillers will keep you guessing (By Death series), and her romantic comedies will keep you giggling (It's a Dog's Life and Charmin Marvin Romantic Comedy series).

She honors the stories that come to her – and some of them are crazy and break all the rules and cross multiple genres!

To go with her fiction, she also writes nonfiction in many different fields with books available on resume writing, companion gardening and the US mortgage system. She has recently published her Career Essentials Series. All her books are available in print and ebook format.

Connect with Dale Mayer Online

Dale's Website – www.dalemayer.com
Twitter – @DaleMayer
Facebook – facebook.com/DaleMayer.author
BookBub – bookbub.com/authors/dale-mayer

Also by Dale Mayer

Published Adult Books:

Psychic Vision Series
Tuesday's Child
Hide 'n Go Seek
Maddy's Floor
Garden of Sorrow
Knock Knock…
Rare Find
Eyes to the Soul
Now You See Her
Shattered
Into the Abyss
Seeds of Malice
Eye of the Falcon
Itsy-Bitsy Spider
Psychic Visions Books 1–3
Psychic Visions Books 4–6
Psychic Visions Books 7–9

By Death Series
Touched by Death
Haunted by Death
Chilled by Death
By Death Books 1–3

Charmin Marvin Romantic Comedy Series

Broken Protocols

Broken Protocols 2

Broken Protocols 3

Broken Protocols 3.5

Broken Protocols 1-3

Broken and... Mending

Skin

Scars

Scales (of Justice)

Broken but... Mending 1-3

Glory

Genesis

Tori

Celeste

Glory Trilogy

Biker Blues

Morgan: Biker Blues, Volume 1

Cash: Biker Blues, Volume 2

SEALs of Honor

Mason: SEALs of Honor, Book 1

Hawk: SEALs of Honor, Book 2

Dane: SEALs of Honor, Book 3

Swede: SEALs of Honor, Book 4

Shadow: SEALs of Honor, Book 5

Cooper: SEALs of Honor, Book 6

Markus: SEALs of Honor, Book 7

Evan: SEALs of Honor, Book 8

Mason's Wish: SEALs of Honor, Book 9
Chase: SEALs of Honor, Book 10
Brett: SEALs of Honor, Book 11
Devlin: SEALs of Honor, Book 12
Easton: SEALs of Honor, Book 13
Ryder: SEALs of Honor, Book 14
Macklin: SEALs of Honor, Book 15
Corey: SEALs of Honor, Book 16
Warrick: SEALs of Honor, Book 17
SEALs of Honor, Books 1–3
SEALs of Honor, Books 4–6
SEALs of Honor, Books 7–10
SEALs of Honor, Books 11–13

Heroes for Hire

Levi's Legend: Heroes for Hire, Book 1
Stone's Surrender: Heroes for Hire, Book 2
Merk's Mistake: Heroes for Hire, Book 3
Rhodes's Reward: Heroes for Hire, Book 4
Flynn's Firecracker: Heroes for Hire, Book 5
Logan's Light: Heroes for Hire, Book 6
Harrison's Heart: Heroes for Hire, Book 7
Saul's Sweetheart: Heroes for Hire, Book 8
Dakota's Delight: Heroes for Hire, Book 9
Tyson's Treasure: Heroes for Hire, Book 10
Jace's Jewel: Heroes for Hire, Book 11
Rory's Rose: Heroes for Hire, Book 12
Brandon's Bliss: Heroes for Hire, Book 13
Liam's Lily: Heroes for Hire, Book 14
North's Nikki: Heroes for Hire, Book 15
Heroes for Hire, Books 1–3
Heroes for Hire, Books 4–6

Heroes for Hire, Books 7–9

SEALs of Steel
Badger: SEALs of Steel, Book 1
Erick: SEALs of Steel, Book 2
Cade: SEALs of Steel, Book 3
Talon: SEALs of Steel, Book 4
Laszlo: SEALs of Steel, Book 5
Geir: SEALs of Steel, Book 6
Jager: SEALs of Steel, Book 7
The Last Wish: SEALs of Steel, Book 8

Collections
Dare to Be You…
Dare to Love…
Dare to be Strong…
RomanceX3

Standalone Novellas
It's a Dog's Life
Riana's Revenge
Second Chances

Published Young Adult Books:

Family Blood Ties Series
Vampire in Denial
Vampire in Distress
Vampire in Design
Vampire in Deceit
Vampire in Defiance
Vampire in Conflict

Vampire in Chaos
Vampire in Crisis
Vampire in Control
Vampire in Charge
Family Blood Ties Set 1–3
Family Blood Ties Set 1–5
Family Blood Ties Set 4–6
Family Blood Ties Set 7–9
Sian's Solution, A Family Blood Ties Series Prequel
    Novelette

Design series
Dangerous Designs
Deadly Designs
Darkest Designs
Design Series Trilogy

Standalone
In Cassie's Corner
Gem Stone (a Gemma Stone Mystery)
Time Thieves

Published Non-Fiction Books:

Career Essentials
Career Essentials: The Résumé
Career Essentials: The Cover Letter
Career Essentials: The Interview
Career Essentials: 3 in 1

Made in the USA
Monee, IL
30 September 2020

43607177R00133